JOANNA BESS

Josephine's Defiance

Image Credit: Zharinova Marina/Shutterstock.com

First edition

ISBN: 978-1-7375466-8-9

Cover art by Elizabeth Hubbard

This book was professionally typeset on Reedsy.
Find out more at reedsy.com

To my family, especially my mom, dad, and J.C. who always support me in everything that I do. Thank you. I love you all.

.

Contents

Preface

I wrote this book because I grew up on the farm where the slave pen, that can now be seen in the National Underground Railroad Freedom Center, used to sit. My mom and I would often walk in the field and talk about what it would have been like to live in the cabin when it was first built as a home, when neighbors would have been miles away and the wilderness was endless. Then, we would talk about the darker side. What it would have been like to be forced to pass through this land in chains, not knowing where you were or where you were going. I would often wonder what it would have been like growing up during that time on the farm and seeing that take place. This book is what I came up with. I hope you enjoy.

Acknowledgement

I'd like to send out a special thanks to my two editors: Chloe Gibson for suffering through my earliest draft and sending me in the right direction and Diana Welte for helping me bring it all together and answering my million and one questions.

I'd also like to thank my cousin, Elizabeth Hubbard, for the beautiful cover art. Thanks for not killing me as I changed my mind multiple times. You are very gifted and I truly appreciate you.

Chapter 1

I hate cities, but I'm not sure why. I was born in Boston. I grew up there, had a loving family and a wonderful childhood, but I still dislike cities. Cities, in general, always feel cold, like they are telling me I don't belong. I long to go south and live in the country. I want to feel the warmth of the sunshine on my face, walk along an old dirt path, feel the grass between my toes, and relax on the porch as the sun slowly sinks below the horizon. To walk through a beautiful garden full of sweet-smelling flowers just to emerge and see vast fields lying before me, that is my dream. Literally, it is in my dreams, almost every night now. This dream started when I was younger, shortly after I found an old drawing of a little boy tucked away in a copy of Oliver Twist that I had picked up at an antique store while visiting family in Philadelphia. I felt drawn to that book and when I opened it, out fell the drawing. I picked it up gently so as not to rip it and studied it. The little boy seemed so familiar to me. The page was ripped in half, so I shook the book, but the other half was not there. I quickly put the drawing back into the book and placed it with the other items my mother was purchasing. If only the little boy in the drawing could talk and tell me why I keep having this dream that is always the same. The dream is so vivid it feels like I know that place, like I am home, but I have never been to the country.

The house in my dreams is two stories and sits on a hill, quite different from the tiny apartments that I have lived in. It is white with green shutters and has a large front porch with a swing. I picture myself relaxing there with an ice-cold sweet tea, listening to the birds sing their happy songs. The dirt lane leading to the house has two shimmering ponds on each side with a land bridge passing over them. The yard is dotted with dandelions and violets, beautiful pine trees, and gardens of peonies, snapdragons, irises, and roses. The dreams are so real that I can smell the sweetness of the flowers, feel the soft breeze against my skin, and hear the buzzing of the bees as they flit from flower to flower. As I walk through the gardens, I can see fields of tobacco and corn surrounding the house. Then, people slowly come into view. They are working in the fields, bent at the waist planting tiny tobacco plants, careful not to damage any part of the fragile plant. They sing a song so melancholy that even I feel as if all hope is lost. Their song starts to pull me in and fill me with their deep sadness. Then, it happens. I hear a voice, unfamiliar yet comforting, call out "Josephine." My heart leaps in my chest and I spin around, but before I can see who it is, I wake up. This happens every time and I am always left with the same unanswered questions: *Where is this place that haunts my dreams and why does it feel like home to me when I have never set foot on its grounds? Who is this person and why do they call me Josephine?*

My name is Samantha. I am in bed, in my apartment, asking myself these questions. I no longer live in an apartment with my parents up north, I have traveled south. But not completely into the south - I have only made it as far as Cincinnati. Yes,

I'm still a city girl, still living in an apartment and still wishing I could move to the country, find the house from my dreams, and maybe figure out why I have this reoccurring dream without an ending. Who is the man and why does he call me Josephine? Does the house even exist? I can't worry about that now, though, I have to get ready for work. The kids would love it if their history teacher was late, but I am afraid the principal would not.

I enjoy teaching history. My favorite time period is the Civil War Era, which is what I have been teaching as of late. This could be why my dream has become more frequent, because it seems to be set in or around that time period. It is the most fascinating time period in American history to me. There are so many different points of view within that time, from the abolitionist of the north to the secessionist of the south to the tortured slave of the field. My mind goes crazy just thinking about brother fighting brother and father fighting son. Slaves being ripped away from their families and bought and sold like cattle. I often wonder what it would have been like to live in that era. Part of me feels like I already know.

I make it into school just as the bell begins to ring. *Shoo, just in time.*

"Hey Samantha, how was your weekend?" My best friend and fellow teacher, Maggie asks.

"I can't talk now, I'll let you know on the bus," I say as I hurry into my classroom.

We are going on a field trip today to the National Underground Railroad Freedom Center. I don't have time to tell her that yet another online dating guy did not look like his profile picture and did not actually enjoy "cooking, animals, and the outdoors." I did get a free Red's game out of the date though,

3

so I can safely say I have had worse. So far, at 25, I have not been able to find anyone that comes close to the type of person I want to spend my life with.

It takes me a few minutes to get the kids quiet, due to field trip excitement, but once I get them under control, I go over the rules for the day and we are off to what will hopefully be a fun day of learning. We arrive at the Freedom Center and the staff takes us to an auditorium that has a ceiling made to look like the night sky. The children are so mesmerized by the stars that the guides have to bribe them with candy to regain their attention. They show a short orientation film that takes us through an overview on what our day at the Freedom Center will entail and all the exhibits we will see. I can't wait. I am probably more excited to explore the Freedom Center than my pupils. After the film, we embark on our journey, navigating through each exhibit. The students are amazing, asking questions and really engaging with each exhibit. The final exhibit is the one I am most interested in viewing - the slave pen.

"This structure was built in the early 1800's on a farm in Mason County, Kentucky by Captain John W. Anderson, a slave trader," the guide began.

I find myself staring at the structure. It looks like a normal log cabin of the time. Two stories high built with large logs and layers of chinking between each log. It also has a huge stone fireplace along with a number of windows and a door. The frightening difference between this structure and a normal log cabin is the fact that this structure has metal bars that dissect the windows into quarters and metal rings nailed by thick stakes into the floorboards on the second floor. The guide explains that slave traders would travel with their slaves about

4

15 miles a day on their journey to an auction and log cabins like these were used to keep the slaves from running away at night. The slaves would be in shackles, fastened to the metal rings, forced to sleep on the cold, wood floor.

"How could any human be so cruel to another?" Maggie whispers.

I shake my head and shrug. I can't understand it either. As I stand toward the back of the group and listen to the story, I start to feel weird. My vision turns hazy and I feel like I am going to pass out. I reach for Maggie.

"Are you ok?" she asks.

"I don't know," I mutter. "I feel kind of faint."

"Did you eat breakfast? I know how you get when you don't eat, all cranky and wiggly." "Yes, I ate breakfast. I always eat breakfast. Toast with apple butter. Ugh, never mind my eating habits. Just make sure I don't fall over in front of the kids."

"Maybe you should sit down."

I can't stand the concerned look on her face. "No, I'm ok, I feel a bit better already," I lie. I don't feel better. There is something strange about this slave pen. It feels oddly familiar to me, but I have no idea why. I want to walk to it, touch it, remember. Remember what? What am I supposed to remember? I feel like I am going insane between this and the dream. I need a vacation. Good thing summer break is just around the corner.

The guide finishes telling us the brief history of the structure and allows us to explore it on our own. As I walk towards it, my heart starts to race. I step inside the slave pen, still dizzy, and place my hand on the smooth log wall to steady myself. I close my eyes willing the feeling away. I can hear the chatter of my middle school students as they explore the large room, talking about how horrible it would be to be chained up like an animal and how this is the most impacting field trip they have ever been on. I smile to myself, glad that they are getting something out of this, when everything suddenly shifts. The wall beneath my hand goes from smooth to rough, the air grows hot and muggy, and the smell of sweat overwhelms my senses. I hear children crying, men shouting, and the clinking of chains. My heart pounds. The feeling of despair weighs so heavily on me that I can't open my eyes. I shouldn't be here.

Then I hear a concerned voice, "Josephine, what are you doing in here?"

"I'm not Josephine, I'm Samantha. I'm Samantha!"

"Sam, we know who you are. Are you ok?" I open my eyes to see Maggie kneeling next to me and my students huddled around her looking worried.

"Are you ok, Miss Worsham?" one of my students, a young boy named Winston asks.

"Yes, I'm fine. I must have just gotten too hot. I'm okay now, thank you." I sit up feeling rather embarrassed and Maggie helps me to my feet. Seeing I was alright, the students gradually wander away to do more exploring. Maggie; however, does not look convinced. She grabs my shoulders and forces me to face her, searching my eyes for an answer.

"What just happened?" she asks.

I look at her and shake my head, unsure of how to explain without sounding nuts. "I don't know. It was like I went back in time. I could hear people crying and the clinking of chains. I felt the despair of being chained with no means of escape."

"That's crazy."

"I know! But it's true. What's even crazier is that someone called me Josephine. That's only happened in my dreams!"

She gives me an imploring look. "Samantha, I think you've been working too hard. You need a vacation."

"What I need is to find out more about this place, where it was and whose it was. I need
answers."

Before I board the bus back to school, I catch up with our guide.

"Thank you so much for taking us through the exhibits today. It seems like the students really enjoyed them."

"I'm so glad everyone enjoyed their time here. How are you feeling?" she asks rather concerned.

"Oh, I'm fine, thank you. I just got a little hot and before I could take off my jacket, I went down. I was wondering if you could give me a little more information about the slave pen."

"Certainly, what would you like to know?"

"Well, where was it originally located and is it possible to visit the grounds there?"

"I don't know the exact address, but I can tell you about where it was located. The last I heard it is still a working farm in Kentucky, so I am not sure if the current owners would allow you to visit the actual site. It is just down the AA highway, between the historic towns of Augusta and Maysville. If you can't see the actual site, exploring those two towns as well as Old Washington in Mason County would be a treat in itself."

"Great, thank you so much. And thanks again for a wonderful day!" I quickly shake her hand and head toward the bus, feeling one step closer to getting some answers.

Back on the bus, I find my seat next to Maggie. "How about a road trip?" I ask.

"You know I'm always up for an adventure. Where to, Columbus, Cleveland, Toledo?"

"No, how about Maysville, Augusta, and Old Washington?"

"Well, they don't sound as glamorous as my choices, but I guess I'll go."

"You may run into George Clooney, I heard that is where he grew up."

"In that case I am definitely in."

I knew that would get her. Maggie loves George Clooney. "Good, we'll leave early

Saturday morning."

"How early is early? You know I hate getting up before 11 AM on Saturdays."

"Oh, stop complaining. You just said you would go. It's supposed to be beautiful this

weekend and you have nothing else to do. I'll pick you up at 8."

"And you'll buy me lunch," she says with a devilish grin.

"You drive a hard bargain, but it's a deal," I say laughing.

Chapter 2

My alarm goes off and my eyes pop open. This is going to be a great Saturday. I can feel it. I swing by and pick up Maggie. The drive down the AA highway is picturesque. Kentucky's gently rolling hills surround us, dotted with trees and flowers in bloom, and cows lazily roaming the fields chewing their cud. We pass a sign that directs us to turn toward Augusta, but our plan is to start at Old Washington, because that town seems to be more historically centered according to my research. Then we will make our way to Maysville and then take in Augusta on our way back home. We reach Old Washington about fifteen minutes later and park near the visitor's center. As soon as we step out of the car, it feels like we are transported back in time.

"This place is amazing," I say to Maggie.

The cobblestone streets are lined with men dressed in tightly tailored coats and trousers and ladies dressed in colorful bell-shaped skirts held out by layers and layers of crinoline. As we walk by them, we can hear them discussing the troubles of their time - slavery.

"Good day," one of the men says tipping his hat as we pass.

"Good day," I reply rather shyly.

Maggie giggles, "This is so cool."

"I know, right? And we just got here! I think this place is

going to be fun."

We walk into the visitor's center, where a plaque informs us that it used to be the home of James Paxton, prominent lawyer and emancipationist. We are met by a woman dressed in a dark green, hooped skirt with even darker green, fringed flounces. Her brown hair is tied up in a bun and tucked neatly under a matching green bonnet.

"Welcome to the Paxton House," she greets. "Would you like to take a guided tour through our lovely town today?"

Maggie and I look at each other for a brief second, before turning to the woman. "Sure," we both say together.

"Great," she says. "We will begin in 15 minutes. Please feel free to wander around the room and have a look at some of the antiques."

"Thank you," I respond.

The room is rather large with every bit of a 12-foot high ceiling, if not higher. The floor is made of large wood planks which meet white walls. Along one of the walls stands a grand fireplace, its wooden mantle covered in intricate floral designs. The craftsmanship is amazing. Across the room hangs some old quilts and several display boxes hold antique buttons that had been found along the grounds of Old Washington. A confederate uniform catches my eye. I walk over to it wondering who wore it, if they survived, and how terrified they must have been to march into battle.

"Sam?"

I am jolted out of my day dream by Maggie calling to me.

"What?"

"Oh good. I thought you were doing that weird thing again where you go back in time."

"Ha ha. Very funny," I say lightly smacking her arm.

"Come on," she whines rubbing her invisible wound, "the tour is getting ready to start."

We meet up with the rest of the group and discover that the gentleman who wished us 'a good day' is going to be our tour guide. He introduces himself as Michael. He looks like quite a dapper gentleman, mutton chops and all. He leads us to the first stop on our tour, Mefford's Fort, an old, authentic log cabin. It was in this cabin, he says, that a Mr. George Mefford, his wife, and 13 children resided in the late 1700's.

"Could you imagine living in that tiny cabin with 13 children?" I ask Maggie.

"We do it everyday teaching 30 some children in our classrooms."

"Good point. No wonder we're a bit crazy!" I exclaim laughing.

Outside the cabin there are several men dressed in buckskin breeches and unbleached linen shirts. Some are busy carving wood while others fashion steel into sharp knives. Inside the cabin we find women wearing much looser fitting and less colorful dresses than the ladies outside the visitor's center, all of them dipping candles and making brooms. Maggie and I try our hand at making a broom, but fail miserably. We each purchase one instead.

We backtrack past the Paxton House and briefly pause by the home of Confederate General Albert Sydney Johnston before arriving at the Marshall Key house. Based on her experiences while staying at this house, Harriet Beecher Stowe wrote *Uncle Tom's Cabin*. It is now the Harriet Beecher Stowe museum. We are led inside as Michael tells us Stowe's story and outlines some of the aspects of slavery she may have witnessed while staying in Old Washington. The next site, a large brick house surrounded by fields, still includes slave quarters that we can see from a distance. It was once owned by Captain Thomas Marshall, first Clerk of the county court and prominent slave owner.

"Would you look at that house," Maggie exclaims in awe. "Isn't it the most impressive house you've ever seen?"

"In real life, yes," I respond. "I've seen lots of houses like these in my history textbooks, though. What I would give to be able to live in one! I would probably feel like royalty."

We continue on our tour, heading for a courthouse lawn where slave auctions were held before the Civil War. The closer we get, the quicker my heart beats. Oh no, I think, not again. I grab Maggie's hand.

"It's happening again, isn't it?" she whispers.

I look at her wide-eyed and nod my head. My pulse continues to climb and my breathing becomes more rapid.

"Here we have the courthouse lawn," Michael begins.

I close my eyes, trying to calm myself down. *Just relax, you're fine.*

I'm not fine, though. Just like before, I feel everything around me start to change. I'm hit with the smell of damp earth, the sound of an auctioneer's voice booming over the chatter of a crowd of people. My skin feels clammy, like I've been soaked by a sudden rain storm. I struggle to draw in a breath as my lungs burn and my heart pounds against my ribcage.

"Benjamin!" I yell.

"Sorry ma'am," someone murmurs rather shyly. "You're too late, he's already gone."

"No, no, he can't be, no!"

"Samantha, Samantha, you're okay, just breathe!"

"I'm too late," I sob. I feel hands on me and I snap back to reality. Maggie has a hold of my shoulders trying to shake me awake.

"You're okay," she assures me.

Tears stream down my face as I try to catch my breath. The other members of the tour group along with Michael stare at me, some with alarm, others bewilderment.

"Oh my goodness, I'm so sorry," I manage to stammer between breaths.

Maggie grabs me by the arm. "If you'll excuse us, I think we will finish the walking tour on our own a bit later," she says as she pulls me away towards the nearest coffee shop. Inside, we head straight for a corner booth where Maggie stares at me from across the table.

"Ok, what the heck was that?"

"I don't know. I started feeling odd. I felt everything change around me, even the weather. There was a crowd of people. It was raining and my clothes were soaked. I was looking for someone. It was imperative that I find him."

"Yeah, I know. I'm pretty sure everyone within three blocks of here knows you were looking for Benjamin."

"I'm so sorry if I embarrassed you. You and our whole group probably think I'm crazy. Heck, I think I am too! Why is this happening to me?"

"Going crazy? Girl, you already were!" Maggie says, chuckling.

"Ha, ha, very funny."

"On a serious note, we have another clue to add to our search. This fellow named Benjamin. Who is he and why is he so important to you?"

"Important to me or Josephine?" Although this is the least of my questions, it's the only one I have the courage to ask in this moment."

"You, Josephine, I'm pretty sure you're one in the same, just from different time periods."

"Now who's crazy?" But I ponder the thought for a minute. "Well, if I have been reincarnated, which is very much against my Catholic upbringing, that still doesn't tell me why my past life is mingling with my present one?"

"I don't know for sure. I've read that things like this can happen because there is some unfinished business in a past life troubling the unconscious mind."

"Whoa Mags, that's deep. So, you're saying the only way I can stop this from happening again is to complete some unfinished business that I may or may not have from a past life that I may or may not have lived?"

"Yep, that's pretty much it."

"Totally crazy. Come on, let's get out of here before I faint again."

"Can't we at least go to a couple antique stores? There are so many, and I saw one called The Strawberry Patch that looked so cute." She flashes her big, blue eyes at me while sticking out her lip.

"How can I say no to puppy dog eyes!" I laugh. "Let's go."

After a few hours of rummaging through antique stores, we decide to grab a bite to eat at a little ice cream shop with the most delicious wraps and ice cream I have ever tasted. As I lick the drippings from my fingers, I see Maggie glance at her phone.

"Oh my gosh, look at the time!" she says shocked. It's already three o'clock.

"This place sends you back in time, but makes the time fly by! We aren't going to be able to hit Maysville and Augusta both today."

"Well, I hear Maysville has some decent nightlife. We can always pop down there after we eat here, do a little sightseeing and shopping. We can check out the Old Pogue distillery, catch a movie at the Old Russell Theatre, and stay the night in a hotel by the river."

"Why do I get the feeling you have been planning that line for a while now?"

"Honey, I've been scoping this trip out since you mentioned it to me on the bus. If we are going to take a road trip, we are going to do it right."

"Yes ma'am, lead the way," I answer in approval, saluting her as we head back to the car.

The drive to Maysville takes us on a curvy road that winds down through a hill thick with trees, lined with daffodils, and several lovely houses. Apparently, according to Maggie's research, it used to be an old buffalo trail.

"I guess buffalo don't know how to walk in straight lines!" Maggie shouts clinging to the door handle.

We arrive downtown and I realize the guide from the museum is not exaggerating: Maysville is a place to see. The shops are great and the town is bordered by a flood wall with paintings depicting the history of the town. The best part, though, has to be the architecture. The Gothic style of a church called St. Patrick catches my eye, while Maggie admires the Federal and Queen Anne style row houses. We walk into the museum and I stop short only to be rear ended by Maggie.

"Wow, Sam, haven't you ever heard you are not supposed to stop in the doorway?"

I ignore that comment as I walk closer to a drawing hanging on the lobby wall.

"This is it Maggie. This is the house in my dreams. It must exist. You see it, right?"

"Yes, but that could be any old farm house around here. You saw them all on the way down here."

"Cecilia," I whisper.

"What?" Maggie asks.

"The signature on the drawing. The artists name is Cecilia."

"May I help you?" A young woman asks as she comes out of the back room.

"Where is this house?" I demand.

"I'm sorry, I don't know. I just moved and started working here recently. I'll check the back and see if there is a sticker or something that may tell us where it came from. Sometimes these things are donated and won't have anything on them," she says as she takes it off the wall. "Here's a sticker. It looks like the Augusta Art Guild."

I glance at my watch. "It's 4:30. I wonder what time they close?"

Maggie holds her cell phone up to my face. "They close at 4:30, but good news, they are open tomorrow."

"Hopefully someone will be able to tell us more information on this house, but until then, let's see what we can find in here."

Chapter 3

"Jo, wake up," someone whispers.

"What?" I say as I try to pry my eyes open. My panic grows when I notice that the mattress beneath me feels hard and the room itself is chilly.

"It will be time to board the boat soon."

"I don't want to go. I belong here, let me stay here."

"You shouldn't have made Mother angry."

"I'm not going! I don't want to go!" I yell.

"Samantha, wake up. You're dreaming, wake up."

I open my eyes slowly and see Maggie staring down at me. This is becoming an all too familiar scene for me.

"You did it again. What was going on this time, where did you not want to go?" she asks.

"I don't know. Someone told Josephine to wake up, that it was time to board the boat. It was so chilly in here."

"Did you see anything? Who were you talking too?"

"I don't know. I couldn't open my eyes and I didn't hear a name."

"You're really not helping this investigation," Maggie complains, sounding disappointed.

"My apologies, but it's not like I have an instruction booklet on how to recall past lives," I point out as I whack her with my pillow. "Believe me, I want to figure this out as well, more than you know. What time is it?" I ask.

"Time to get up and go. We have a mystery to solve," she commands as she retaliates with a pillow shot to my head.

"Calm down Nancy Drew. I need to get some food in me before we go. I don't know if Josephine is in my past, but complimentary breakfast is definitely in my future. Besides, I think these flashbacks are wearing me out, I'm exhausted! Hopefully we can find answers in Augusta, because I don't know how much more of this I can take."

The drive to Augusta, which follows along the Ohio River, is picturesque. The sun sparkling off the river and the trees waving in the breeze make for a breathtaking view.

"I absolutely love this area," I comment as we drive.

"Me too," Maggie responds lazily as she gazes out the window.

"Really? I thought you were more of a big city girl."

"I know, right? I was afraid I was going to be bored out of my mind, but this area is so charming. I can't believe we haven't visited it before now. As shocked as I am to be saying this, I think I could actually live here."

"Wow! That is saying a lot for you. I'm glad you're enjoying this trip and I am so glad you agreed to come with me."

"You're my best friend! Where you go, I go, even if it means the possibility of being bored to tears," she says laughing.

We make it to Augusta in good time and start off by wandering around aimlessly in search of the art guild and taking in the sights and sounds. The day is another beautiful, sunny day with only a few wispy, white clouds in the sky. The houses are beautiful, massive in size with nice, wooden porches. After walking along a beautiful street canopied by shade trees, we reach the Augusta Art Guild. We step into the quirky shop and start to wander through the exhibits. Several talented local artists are on display.

"I wish I could bring nature to life through a drawing, don't you Maggie?"

"Absolutely. I can't even draw a straight line with a ruler!"

"I hear you."

Someone nearby chuckles. I look over and smile. Standing near us is an eccentric lady with dark hair that is graying, mostly in a streak across the top, giving her the appearance of a skunk. I giggle to myself.

"Hello," she greets. "Welcome to our guild."

"Hi, all of the art here is beautiful."

"Thank you, we do our best here in this little town."

"Well, this town is very nice. It feels so familiar to me, yet I've never been here before."

"Really, where are you from?"

"We both teach in Cincinnati. I teach history and Maggie teaches English."

"That's wonderful. What brings you here?"

"Well, we were in Maysville yesterday and came across a drawing of a house and the sticker on the back was from here. The artists name is Cecilia. Do you know her or where I can find that house?"

"I do know Cecilia, lovely lady and successful artist. The house she drew is probably the one she is opening up for a bed and breakfast soon. Take a look at the flyers over on the corkboard. I think she has one over there. Please sign our guest book as well."

"We definitely will," I assure her. "And what is your name?"

"Diana."

"Thanks Diana! Have a wonderful day."

I walk quickly over to the corkboard, my eyes bouncing from one flyer to another. Then I see it. It is the same drawing of the house that is in the museum.

Opening soon: Newly renovated antebellum home. Come stay with us and enjoy beautiful farmland and delicious food. Taking reservations now.

"They had me at delicious food," Maggie giggles. "This is amazing." She looks at me. "Why aren't you excited?"

"I am. I'm just shocked. I really didn't expect to find anything on this trip, yet here I am staring at this piece of paper with *the* house on it." The significance starts to hit me. "Oh my gosh, this is crazy. This is amazing. I can't believe we found it. I can't believe it's a bed and breakfast." I look around and realize I'm talking to no one because Maggie has walked away. She is talking excitedly on the phone, probably to one of her many boyfriends. Unlike me, she always manages to find one, or two, or three.

I turn back to look for a number or an address on the flyer. I have to see it, not just on paper, but in real life. The next thing I know Maggie is back at my side.

"I got it," she says.

"Got what?" I ask absently.

"A reservation, silly. We are the first people to call. It doesn't open until June and we are staying there for a whole week."

I smile at her and hug her tight.

"Maggie, you are the best friend a woman could ever have. Thank you so much," I manage to choke with tears in my eyes.

"You're very welcome. Now let's go eat," she says with a wink.

Chapter 4

The weeks after our trip feel like they will never end, like June is determined to never arrive. I feel like a child waiting for Christmas. I even go as far as placing a star on the calendar and marking off the days until our trip.

Finally, the day arrives and what a dreary day it is. The clouds are dark and ominous, hanging low to the ground. Lightning flashes and rain pelts our windshield relentlessly. Fittingly, Elvis Presley's "Kentucky Rain" begins playing on the radio. Maggie sings away and although I love Elvis, I really wish the rain would stop. The thought crosses my mind that maybe this wasn't a good idea. Maybe the rain is a sign of things to come. I quickly push the thought out of my mind, turn the windshield wipers up to high, grip the steering wheel a bit too tightly, and push the accelerator down. I need answers and our destination holds that answer, I'm sure of it.

The rain finally dies down to a drizzle as we cross the county line, the GPS returning to life just in time to tell us where to turn. We follow the road for a short distance and then, just as the sun finally breaks through the clouds, I see it. The house from my dreams is perched on top of the hill. It looks regal with the sun shining above it and the raindrops glistening in the light. I turn onto the lane and just as in my dreams, we drive over a land bridge nestled between two ponds. I can see pine trees standing sentry on both sides of the house, while maple and buckeye trees dot the yard. We pull into the gravel driveway and park the car.

Maggie hops out of the car, but I hesitate. "Are you coming or are you just going to sit in the car all week?"

"I still can't believe we found this place. I still can't believe it exists."

"Well it does, so let's go."

I get out of the car and we head towards the front door, passing several flower gardens. The smell of rose, lilac, and peony drifts towards us, and the bees appear busy at work. We step up onto a porch that spans the whole front of the house, admiring the woodwork above us.

"Someone spent a lot of time carving that ginger breading," I say admiringly.

We reach the front door.

"Do we knock or just walk in?" I ask. "It doesn't seem like anyone is home."

"Good question. I think this is an old-fashioned door bell," Maggie answers.

In the middle of the front door was a wrought iron handle.

"It does resemble something I saw in a text book once." I reach out, grab it, and give it a pull downwards. We hear a loud ding. "I believe you were right Maggie."

In an instant, someone opens the door. Standing before us is an elderly woman with a tiny, but strong frame. She smiles. "May I help you?" she asks sweetly.

"Yes ma'am, we have reservations here for this week. This is Maggie and I'm Samantha."

The woman looks at me intently with her golden-brown

eyes before a smile spreads across her face. "Yes," she says, barely above a whisper. "We have been waiting for you." Then she smiles at Maggie and motions for us both. "I'm Cecilia. Please, come inside," she beckons. "Where is your luggage?"

"It's still in the car. We wanted to make sure we were at the right place first," Maggie explains. Although we both knew from my reaction that this was the right place.

We walk from the porch into the entryway. The ceilings stand twelve feet high, and a large, decorative staircase curves up to the second floor. To the left is a sitting room, wicker furniture with blue cushions arranged cozily around the edges. I spot a window seat full of comfy pillows in one of the massive windows that I cannot wait to sink into with a good book. To the right is the dining room, equipped with a massive oak dining table and chairs, matching hardwood floors, and a glistening chandelier. Just beyond that room is a kitchen full of everyday amenities. We notice a closed door on the far wall that Cecilia says sections off the wing where her and her grandson, Theo, live. Her grandson should be home any minute and he will take our bags to our rooms.

"Speaking of your rooms, follow me upstairs and I will show you where they are," she directs.

We follow her up the staircase holding onto the mahogany railing, the surface cool and smooth under my hand. That was something I noticed about this house. Despite the lack of air conditioning and with the June rain creating a thick mugginess in the air outside, every room in the house feels cool and comfortable. *Whoever built this house knew how to catch the breeze,* I thought.

We reach the landing and find a small sitting area at the top between the two bedrooms. Cecilia tells us that we will be the only guests here this week as a trial run, but once she is sure that she and Theo can accommodate multiple guests, she will open up more of the rooms upstairs. There are five total bedrooms and each is large enough to contain its own master bath! I choose the bedroom to the left and step inside where I am met with cheery, white walls, a beautiful blue and white bedspread, and white lace curtains.

"I feel like I'm surrounded by the summer sky on a clear day with traces of puffy, white clouds," I exclaim. "And it smells so fresh and clean."

Maggie's room is decorated in greens and yellows. The bedspread is white with sunflowers, while the sheer curtains are a soft yellow and the carpet is a deep green. Pictures of various yellow flowers accent the light, green walls.

Cecilia hands me a paper. "The wi-fi password is on this paper as well as a list of things to do and see in the surrounding towns and here on the farm. If you have any questions or if you need anything, please don't hesitate to ask. I know this is advertised as a bed and breakfast, but please join my grandson and me at every meal if you are home. Breakfast is at eight, lunch is around noon, and supper is at five. And of course, snacks before bed," she adds with a wink.

"Thank you so much, that's very kind," I reply.

"Oh, Theo is home. I'll have him bring your bags up."

"That's ok," I say as we hear the door downstairs open. "We can get them."

"Nonsense," she waves us off as she turns to head down the stairs.

Maggie grabs my arm and I turn to see her looking at me wide-eyed.

"What?" I ask bewildered by her intensity.

"That woman knows things."

"What do you mean?"

"Didn't you hear what she said out on the porch? She looked straight at you and said we've been waiting for you."

"We did make a reservation, Maggie."

"I know, but you're not getting it. She looked at you when she said it, her stare was fixed on you. And she knew Theo was here before the door even slammed. She knows things."

"Maybe you're right, but I'm not going to interrogate her on our first night here and you're not either, okay?"

Before she can answer, I hear footsteps behind us, so I turn around and see a handsome man about six-foot-tall with broad shoulders carrying our bags. He smiles at both of us, puts our bags down and introduces himself as Theo. He looks so familiar to me, like I've seen him before. I'm trying to figure out where when Maggie nudges me from behind to shake me back to life. Theo is staring at me in awe. Maggie extends her hand.

"I'm Maggie," she introduces herself.

Theo shakes her hand, but never takes his eyes off me. I look away, unable to hold his stare. It makes me a bit uneasy, especially after what Maggie has just said about Cecilia.

"I'm sorry, please forgive me for staring," he apologizes as he offers his hand to me.

"That's okay. I'm Samantha, it's nice to meet you."

Our hands touch and I instantly feel a tingling sensation run up my arm as my heart starts to beat faster. I look into his eyes and the next thing I know I'm staring up at the ceiling. Maggie is leaning over me looking alarmed.

"Are you okay?" she asks.

"Yes, I feel fine. What happened?"

I can see Theo hovering over her shoulder looking concerned. I sit up quickly.

"I'm sorry. I guess the excitement of the trip just got to me. I'm fine, really."

After a few more reassurances that I am okay, Theo leaves to help his grandmother in the flower garden.

"What happened, what did you see?" Maggie excitedly begins her interrogation.

"Nothing, I didn't see anything. I felt weird like I always do before something crazy happens and the next thing I know I'm looking up at you."

"Hmmm, that's disappointing."

"Sorry to disappoint," I say rolling my eyes and shaking my head. "Come on, let's unpack."

Chapter 5

I wake up to a much prettier day than yesterday. The birds are perched in the trees chirping and I can see a hint of pink sky beginning to form as the sun slowly starts to come into view. The open window allows the smell of peonies and lilac to drift into my room, so I breathe in deeply as I sit up in bed. I creep over to Maggie's room and peak in. She is still sleeping, so I decide to get dressed and head downstairs on my own.

I walk into the kitchen to find Cecilia already up and about.

"Good morning, Cecilia."

"Good morning, Samantha. I didn't expect you to be up so early. Did you sleep well?"

"Yes ma'am, it was probably the best night's sleep I've had in a while."

"That's good. If you don't mind me asking, why haven't you been sleeping well?" she asks as she hands me a cup of tea.

Normally, I don't open up so quickly to strangers, but Cecilia has a familiarity about her, just like this house and Theo.

"It's not that I don't sleep well as far as tossing and turning, but I have this recurring dream that always ends the same and wakes me up. It has become more and more frequent. Now that I think about it, though, I didn't have it last night."

"Oh? Dreams are sometimes our subconscious coming

through trying to tell us something that our waking mind cannot comprehend. Tell me about your dream."

"You may think I'm crazy after I tell you."

"No child, I promise you I won't. People often tell me I'm crazy because I sense things that others can't. You are special, Samantha. I sensed that yesterday before I even met you."

"Okay, here goes. I dream about this house, this exact house with flower gardens even more magnificent than they are now. Everything feels so real that I can actually smell the flowers and hear the buzzing of the bees. I look out onto fields and there are people, who appear to be slaves, planting tobacco. Then a man behind me says a name. It's not my name, but it feels like my name. Before I can turn around to see who it is, I wake up."

"What is the name that you hear, dear?"

"He calls me Josephine."

A loud bang interrupts our conversation.

I jump. "What was that?"

Theo comes through the door. "I'm sorry I startled you, I dropped my boots. I was planning on putting them on outside so as not to track dirt everywhere, but it appears that I failed at that," he says slightly embarrassed. "I'll clean it up grandmother, don't worry."

"I know you will, because I didn't make that mess," she replies with a smile on her face.

Theo quickly cleans the mud, grabs a freshly baked biscuit while kissing his grandmother on the cheek, and waves to me as he takes off outside.

"He's a good man," she says lovingly. "He has helped me so much around here, getting this place ready to open."

"May I ask how long you have lived here?"

"I've lived in this area my whole life, but here, I acquired this place about a year ago from my old friend, Eleanor. She wrote me into her will. We had been friends since we were school age and she knew that my ancestors lived here as slaves and that it always brought me closer to them being here. This place was not so easy for them and it breaks my heart to think about what they had to go through, but I feel close to them here and I love this house. I hope to bring this place back to how it used to be with the pristine gardens and such, but I want it to be a happy and safe place for all. For a house and land this beautiful with so much history, it doesn't need to rot and be forgotten."

"It is very beautiful here. I am glad that I finally found it. Since your ancestors lived here, you must know a lot of the history. Did you ever hear anyone mention the name Josephine?"

Cecilia quickly stands up from her chair, not answering my question. "Cecilia, you know something don't you?"

She turns and looks at me with tears forming in her eyes. She opens her mouth to speak, just as Maggie groggily stumbles into the room.

"Something smells delicious," she sighs.

"How did you sleep?" Cecilia asks quickly.

"Like a rock. Everything is quiet here. There were no ambulances screaming by or noisy people. I always thought I was a big city girl, but this quiet country is starting to change my mind."

"I am glad to hear it. Please, sit down. I was just about to serve Samantha up a plate of breakfast. What would you all like? I have fixed eggs, biscuits and gravy, grits, and bacon."

Maggie and I look at each other, thinking the same thing.

This place is the best. "We will have a little of everything, thank you."

Chapter 6

"What do you want to do now?" Maggie asks as we step out onto the porch into the morning sunshine.

"I want to see if I can find out any information about Josephine. Maybe we can hit up the library or search the records at the court house. Maggie, I told Cecilia about my dream. I asked her if she had heard of someone named Josephine and she deliberately ignored my question. I pushed her a little bit more and it seemed like she was about to speak until you walked in."

"Oh, sorry, bad timing on my part."

"That's okay. We are here and we will get answers. I was kind of hoping I would have more visions since I was here, but other than passing out with Theo, there has been nothing, not even last night while I slept."

"Maybe Theo knows something. I'm sure spending a little time with him wouldn't hurt," Maggie says while nudging me.

"Ha, ha. He is very handsome and he seems sweet, but you know what that means?"

"That he's perfect for you?"

"No, he's already taken."

"No, he's not."

"How do you know?"

"You're not the only one who has had time alone with Cecilia."

"Did you seriously ask if her grandson was taken?"

"Yes ma'am, I did. I told her I was just trying to be a good friend to you and I needed to know."

"Oh my gosh, Maggie! How did she react to that? I'm surprised she hasn't kicked us out yet."

"She laughed. Come to think of it, she said something odd."

"What?"

"She said no, he wasn't taken, but then she said his heart is destined for one person only and 'when they fully connect again, two different worlds will become one.'"

"That is really weird. What do you think she meant by that?"

"I have no idea other than he is single, so go connect with him."

Out of words, I just shake my head.

Maggie and I start our search at the library and find quite a bit of information on the local history, but nothing that answers any of my questions. We decide to head to the courthouse next and after several hours of searching the endless shelves of records, we still come up empty-handed.

"I don't understand. I know that this Josephine was real. I could tell by how Cecilia reacted when I said her name. Why can't I find anything?" I whined.

"We are looking for a needle in a haystack. I mean, we don't exactly know what we are looking for other than someone named Josephine. Not exactly a plethora of information there," Maggie states.

"Are you ladies finished?" The clerk asks. "We are getting ready to close."

"Yes ma'am, all finished. Thank you," we both respond

together.

We head out of the court house, both of us starving. Not wanting to inconvenience Cecilia with cooking us supper, we stop to eat before going back to the farm. Since the heat of the day is over, we decide to take a walk around to explore the flower gardens and the walking trail.

"So, this place really looks like your dream?" Maggie asks.

"Yes, the flower gardens are not quite as extravagant as they are in my dream, but they're pretty close. Of course, the house seems a bit more worn and the trees are taller with some of them missing, but yes, it is like my dream."

"That is amazing. Have you had anymore feelings or visions?"

"No, which I don't understand. The weeks leading up to our stay, I was having them every night, but now that we're here, they have completely stopped."

"Maybe your whole purpose was just to find this place."

"But why? I feel like there has to be more, but I have no more clues to go on. This is

frustrating. I thought that by finding this house, this land, I would have answers, but there is nothing. What if I never figure it out?"

"Relax, Samantha, we will find your answers. Right now, look at all the beauty that is surrounding us. We have grass beneath our feet instead of concrete and there are flowers, trees, and fresh air around us. This was just our first day and we have several more to go. We will find your answers before our trip is over, I promise."

"I'm glad one of us is positive, because not even getting a lead from our search in town really put a damper on my outlook."

"It'll be fine, trust me. Now let's walk and enjoy our first evening of peace, it'll do you some good."

Maggie was right. By the time we make it back to the house the sun has set, leaving an orange glow along the horizon, and I find myself feeling relaxed and happy. Cecilia and Theo are on the front porch discussing their day as we walk up. "Did you have a nice walk? Would you like a cup of tea? How about some chocolates?" Cecilia asks.

"Yes, yes, and yes, please," I say laughing.

"Do you have any more questions for them?" Theo teases his grandmother.

"What did you two get into in town?" she asks.

"Grandmother!" Theo says shaking his head with the hopes of silencing her.

"I'm old," she answers with a wink. "I have a right to be nosy.

"It's quite alright," I assure her as I look at Maggie. "I know some of us have already asked questions that should not have been asked."

"What?" Maggie asks innocently.

"We went to the library and the court house looking for any information on the woman in my dream."

"Did you find anything?" Theo asks intently.

"No, nothing, which is quite annoying. Maybe I am crazy and all of this is just in my head."

"Have you had any more visions?"

I look at him puzzled, "How do you know about my visions?"

I turn to Maggie and she returns my gaze apologetically. "I'm sorry, Sam. When you passed out yesterday. I told him that occasionally you had visions. I'm sorry, I was worried."

"No, I haven't had any visions and I didn't have my recurring dream last night. It's the first time in days that I haven't had it. I thought that once I was here everything would fall into place and my questions would be answered, but so far, and I know it has only been a day, absolutely nothing has happened."

"Sometimes," Cecilia pipes in, "you just have to let things happen. Stop trying so hard and let your subconscious take over."

I ponder this as we drink our tea and enjoy some chocolates. Maybe I have been trying too hard, constantly thinking about finding answers and spending the majority of the day searching books for answers that I probably already hold deep down inside. I need to relax and let it happen. Let the answers come to me instead of me finding them.

The crickets begin to chirp and the night breeze carries the smell of lilac and magnolia to us as we sit on the porch enjoying what is left of the evening. Maggie yawns next to me and even though I hate to turn in, I am exhausted as well. We wish Theo and Cecilia a good night and head upstairs.

"What do you say we go to Augusta tomorrow and see what else the town has to offer? Maybe we will run into that quirky artist Diana again. I'd like to talk to her some more, she was very pleasant," Maggie suggests as she crawls into bed.

"That's okay with me. It'll be a good distraction to help relax my mind. I'm going to grab a quick drink. Do you want anything from the kitchen?"

"No thanks," Maggie mumbles already half asleep. "Goodnight."

"Goodnight," I answer as I slip quietly out of her room and down the stairs.

As I descend the stairs, I can hear Cecilia and Theo out on the porch discussing something. Theo sounds rather agitated, while Cecilia seems as calm as usual. As I continue to quietly make my way down each step, I start to make out their words.

"Why can't we just tell her?

"That is not how it works, Theo, and you know it. She would not fully believe it anyway. What if someone had just come right out and told you everything before you were ready, would you have believed it?"

"No, I wouldn't have. I would have thought it was crazy. I did think I was crazy going through the dreams and visions until you helped me open up to our gift of knowing. Samantha already knows something is up, though. She is aware of her dreams and she has had other visions too, just like I did. Why can't you help her along as you did me?"

"I merely explained to you that you had a gift. I told you to relax and accept with your heart what you were seeing and feeling. It wasn't until you opened the full story yourself that I discussed everything with you."

"I know, but why is it taking her so long? When did you learn about everything?"

"My sense is very strong. I knew the minute I stepped onto this property who I was. I saw everything the first time I visited my friend Eleanor here. That is why she left me this place. She said it belonged to me. Now, Samantha knows something, but she is not fully aware yet. When she has fully made the connection, then we can explain everything. Until then, we say nothing, do you understand?"

"But what if she never gets out of her own way. What if she never realizes it?"

"Hush, Theo. Is she not here? Has she not made it this far without any help from us? She will find her way, but it must be on her own."

I stand in the darkness as I process this with a death grip on the banister, barely breathing. Theo and Cecilia both know something. I forget about getting a drink and turn to head quietly back to my room. *What connection am I supposed to make? Why do I even have a connection to this place?* I flop onto my bed face down and take a deep breath. I don't know how much more of this I can take. I roll back over, desperate to think rationally about the situation. Cecilia keeps saying I must get out of my own way and let things happen, but how do I do that? I find myself pondering this for hours, unable to escape my mind. The birds start to sing and the sun is peeking over the horizon by the time I realize that running away is not going to help. The answers are here on this farm and running off to Augusta or Maysville is not going to help me put two and two together. My answers are here and this is where I need to stay until I find them.

Chapter 7

"Samantha? Are you going to get up sometime today?"

I spring up. "What time is it?"

"It's ten o'clock."

I immediately hop out of bed and start throwing clothes on.

"What's the matter with you?"

"I'm wasting time. I didn't mean to sleep this late."

"It's okay, the shops aren't going anywhere, we have time. I was just concerned, because you never sleep in this late."

"I'm sorry, Maggie, but I'm not going shopping with you today. The answers I need are here on this farm and I am going to find them."

"Ok, but what happened to relaxing?"

"Last night, I went down to get some water. I heard Theo and Cecilia talking. They were talking about me! There is some connection that I have with this place."

"Yeah, we already know that."

"I know, but they were talking about their gift of knowing. Theo had visions and dreams like me and Cecilia has a sense so strong she knew who she was the minute she set foot here! The answers I need are here and I am not leaving this place until I find them."

"What do you mean who she was?"

"Are you saying maybe the past life stuff I was telling you about could be real?

"I don't know. I don't know what to think, but I know my answers are here."

"Do you want me to stay and help?"

"No, I think I might be better off on my own today."

"Alright," she says as she hugs me. "Be careful."

"I will."

I grab a bite of breakfast before taking off outside to find Theo. I find him in the garden.

"Good morning," I greet him.

"Good morning," he returns with a smile. "Is there something I can help you with?"

Yes, I think to myself, *tell me everything.* "I was actually hoping I could help you today, if that's okay? I'd like to experience real farm life."

"Yes, of course. I would love to have your company. I am hoeing these pesky weeds right now. Grab a pair of gloves and a hoe from the shed."

Thank goodness I know what a hoe is, but as far as what are plants and what are weeds, I have no idea.

Theo must be able to see my confusion, because he comes over and starts showing me the plants and telling me what each one is. The first job he gives me is to hoe around the tomatoes, which makes it easier for me to tell plant from weed because there are cages around them. He takes the next row over and we work in silence for a while. I notice how quickly and efficiently he works compared to my clumsiness. He looks at me and smiles, "What's wrong?"

"I was just admiring your hoeing skills," I blurt out immediately scolding myself for how stupid that sounded.

He laughs, "I've been doing this a long time."

"What did you do before your grandmother inherited this place?"

"I actually still do it. I am a farrier. Luckily, I am able to still keep doing what I love as well as help my grandmother."

"Have you lived in this area your whole life?"

"Yes, I grew up not too far from here. I always admired this house and land and thought how great it would be to live here with a number of horses and now I am. It's so peaceful now."

"What do you mean now?"

He looks deep into my eyes like he is trying to tell me something, but only shakes his head. "This place has a history as most things do. Growing up here at one time for a man with my skin color would not have been easy."

"I understand. I'm sorry. I teach history and that time period is my favorite to teach for some odd reason. For the life of me, I cannot understand how people thought it was right to buy and sell people and treat them like animals. I will never understand it."

He smiles, "You never did."

"What?" I ask puzzled by the past tense.

"Oh, you never did that...plant," he says quickly as he hurries to the next row.

We continue working our way through the rows of tomatoes and then start on the rows of corn. It is nearing noon and the sun is beating down on us. Theo straightens up, stretches, and pulls his shirt off.

"My goodness," I whisper under my breath. I can count his abs. His muscles flex with every movement and the sweat trickling down his body glistens in the sun. I can't stop staring. Then, I feel it coming on. My heart starts to beat faster and my mood changes. I feel a deep sadness mixed with anger and frustration. The distance between Theo and me grows, as if I am watching him from afar.

"This is not right, he should not be punished this way, he should not be punished at all!" I scream in between sobs.

"Samantha, Samantha, it's okay, just relax."

My eyes flutter open to see Theo peering down at me.

"What happened?" I mumble.

"You tell me. What's my name?"

"It's Theo," I respond quizzically. "That was a weird question, usually I'm asked what my name is or what day it is or something like that."

"Sorry, that's the first question that came to me," he says, seemingly disappointed. "Let's get you to some shade."

He scoops me up in his arms and I can feel myself blushing as I wrap my arms around his neck.

Cecilia comes out onto the porch and hands me an ice-cold lemonade. "Are you okay, sugar?"

"Much better now, thank you. I am not used to manual labor, I guess."

"I have made a few sandwiches if you two would like something to eat."

She brings them out to us and we eat on the porch as the breeze cools us and the robins bounce around in the yard chasing bugs.

After lunch, we finish hoeing the garden and then head to the stable to check on the horses. The smell of horses and fresh hay meet my nose as we walk into the stable. Theo hands me an apple and is shocked when he learns that I have never been this close to a horse before. I'm quite nervous, because I hear they can bite hard. Theo reassures me that everything will be okay. Apple in hand, I walk toward the horse's stall. She peers out at me and whinnies. I jump back startled, right into Theo's strong arms. He laughs and whispers in my ear to not be afraid. My heart skips a beat, but not because of the horse. I step up to the stall again with Theo close behind me. He grabs my hand and tells me to hold the apple flat in my palm. I offer the apple up to the horse with Theo's hand right under mine. The horse chomps away at the apple, but I barely even notice it. My mind is drifting to places it should not be. I turn around and look up at Theo. He is so close, his eyes searching mine. I barely know him, but all of this feels right. My hands slide up his arms, feeling the muscles tense as his arms slide around my waist, pulling me closer to him.

"There you are," Maggie says as she comes barging into the stable. "I've been looking all over for you. I had the best day today," she adds as Theo and I quickly separate.

"I'll see you this evening, Samantha. Maggie as well if she wants to come along," Theo says as he exits the stable.

"Did I interrupt something?" Maggie questions looking at me sideways.

"No, he was just showing me the horses."

"Right. What are you two doing tonight?"

"We are all going horseback riding this evening."

"That sounds like fun, but are you sure you want me to come?"

"Yes, please come," I grab her arm and give her my best puppy dog eyes. "I can't be alone with him again. I don't know what came over me just now. I never act like that. I don't even know him! But for some reason, being with him, it just feels right."

After a supper of burgers and hot dogs right off the grill along with all the fixings, we head out to saddle up our horses.

I choose Molly, the mare that scared me silly earlier. She is about ten years old and chestnut in color. I like how soft her nose feels when she nuzzles my hand, looking for more apples, I'm sure. Maggie picks a grey stallion named Anderson and Theo goes with his favorite black and white filly named Shadow.

"Shadow," I repeat softly. That rings a bell, but once again I don't know why. We have a nice ride down the lane and around the pond, the frogs serenading us as we pass. A blue heron peers at us uncertainly from across the pond and several muskrats swim lazily on their backs, causing ripples to form in the water. We continue on deeper into the woods where we see the white tails of three deer as they bound away from us. We exit the woods as the setting sun casts a glow across the fields. I know in this moment that I never want to leave. It beats the city a hundred times over and I've only been here a short time. We make it back to the stable and help Theo take care of each horse, giving them lots of head scratches and treats. Once each horse has been properly cared for, we head back to the house. I feel exhausted and sore from the day's work and desperate to crawl into bed. I wish everyone a goodnight, climb the stairs to my room, and fall into bed willing sleep to overcome me.

Thunk, thunk, thunk. I sit up in bed. *Thunk thunk thunk.* Still in a haze, I listen quietly, trying to figure out who or what could be making that noise. It sounds like it is coming from the closet. *Could be a mouse,* I think doubtfully. I reach for my phone, my body aching from the previous day's work, it's 3:00 AM. *Thunk, thunk, thunk.* I try to go back to sleep, but find it impossible. I slowly get out of bed, muscles screaming with every movement. What I am going to do when I find out what is making that noise, I have no idea. I open the closet door and the noise stops. I shine my phone light all over the closet, moving my clothes and shoes around to see better. I see what looks like an old piece of paper, brown and brittle, stuck between the floor board and the wall. I push along the board and it wiggles a little. I grab my keys and pry the board up gently. It comes up easily. Underneath the board is a small space with what appears to be a few child's items in it. What I thought was a brown piece of paper sticking up is a piece of a doll made out of cornhusk. It looks pretty worn and I am surprised it has not completely disintegrated. No telling how long it has been hidden here! I decide to wait until morning to tell Cecilia what I have found, so she can decide what to do with the items. At the same time, though, I feel drawn to the doll. It seems familiar to me. I pick it up carefully so as not to crumble it and begin to examine it. "Why do you seem so familiar to me?" I whisper to it. When no answers come, I lean forward to put it back where I found it and as I do, beady, little mouse eyes meet mine. "Eeeek!" I jump backwards, tripping over a pair of shoes, and hit my head. Everything goes black.

Chapter 8

August 1850, Kentucky

I spring up out of bed. The sun is just peeking over the horizon and the birds are beginning to sing their morning songs. *Today is my tenth birthday!* I go to my secret hiding place and grab the doll that Benjamin gave me last night for my present. It is a doll made out of cornhusks, but I don't care, it came from my best friend and I love it. I give her a hug and tuck her back underneath the floor board. I can't let my mother see it, she hates that I play with Benjamin and would probably destroy the doll if she knew about it. She wouldn't understand why I want to play with such a doll when I have fancy, china dolls to play with. I like the cornhusk doll the best because it is different and Benjamin made it for me. Benjamin has been my best friend my whole life. His mother, Ann, took care of both of us when we were little, so we played together every day. My father bought Ann for my mother right before she gave birth to me and now that Benjamin and I are older, Ann just takes care of my mother.

"What are you doing out of bed so early?" Millie spits as she enters my room.

Millie belongs to me. My father bought her for me when I was six so that Ann could give all of her attention to my mother's needs. Millie is only about four years older than me, but she doesn't act like a kid at all. She never wants to play with me and when she fixes my hair, she always pulls so hard and hurts my head. If I cry out, she pulls even harder, so I've learned to keep quiet. I told mother that Millie pulls my hair when she brushes it and she hit Millie with the hair brush over the head several times and then told me I would have to learn to control my own slave. I never have said another word to my mother about it. I don't like Millie much, but I don't want to see her get hurt. Mother's beating didn't do any good anyway, it just made Millie hate me more and pull harder.

I ignore Millie as she goes about her business emptying my chamber pot and making my bed.

"Happy birthday my beautiful girl," Mother says as she hands me a package. "I knew you would be up early. I will give you my present now and your father will give you his after we eat breakfast."

I open the package quickly. Inside is a beautiful black riding habit, which can only mean one thing. I hug mother tightly and quickly start to get dressed with Millie's help.

"Please Millie, hurry!" I exclaim barely able to hold in my excitement.

I rush downstairs to the dining room and am extremely happy that breakfast is already on the table.

"Good morning, Josephine. May I ask why you are up so early and where you got that fancy attire?" my father asks with a twinkle in his eye. "It looks good with your auburn hair."

"It's my birthday, Daddy! Mother got this for me. She said you had a present for me too. Can we see it now?"

46

"I'm afraid my present will have to wait until after you eat breakfast. You wouldn't want to upset Frannie by not eating this wonderful meal she made for you."

"Happy birthday, little missy. I made your favorite this morning, pancakes and grits," Frannie says beaming with pride as she stands in the corner.

Pancakes and grits are my favorite and I love Frannie very much, but I really just want to see my other present. I can't disobey though, so I sit down and begin to eat. "Thank you Frannie, these are very good."

"Josephine, you don't thank Frannie. She is too ignorant to understand what you are saying," Mother scolds.

I glance at Frannie and I can see sadness in her eyes.

I look away. "Yes ma'am," I quietly agree.

My brother, John, comes bounding into the dining room. He is three years older than me, tall and thin with brown hair.

"Happy birthday," he says with a wide grin on his face.

"Thank you," I say beaming. Although John is older than me, he is the best brother a sister could have. He doesn't tease me much and if there are things I don't understand, he always finds a better way to explain them to me. I love him dearly.

I eat my food as fast as I can, but not so quickly that my mother will scold me for being unlady-like. It doesn't matter really, because I have to wait for everyone to finish eating their breakfast. My father is talking to John about all the work that needs to be done today, laying out a never-ending list.

Finally, Father looks up, "Are you ready for your present now, Josephine?"

"Yes," I squeal excitedly.

He holds his arm out for me, "My lady."

Giggling, I take it and he escorts me out the front door. The morning sun and the smell of magnolia hit me as we step out onto the front porch. It is a beautiful day; it is *my* day. Once my eyes adjust to the early morning sunlight, I see her. She is the most beautiful pony I have ever seen. She has a shiny black coat with a patch of white on her chest like a shield. She is already saddled up and ready for me to ride. Benjamin is at her front holding her harness with a smile on his face. Benjamin loves horses and I overheard my parents saying that he would not be moved to the fields, but would continue to learn from Tom and eventually take his place when he gets too old to work. That news made my heart leap for joy.

I walk over to the pony and put my hand out. She nuzzles it gently. Her nose is soft and her warm breath tickles my skin.

"What are you going to name her?" Mother asks.

"Shadow," I declare without hesitation. "I am going to name her Shadow."

The horse whinnies as if in approval.

John helps me into the saddle, Benjamin hands me the reins, and the next thing I know, my father is next to me on his horse, Bandit. He is named Bandit because he is always trying to steal treats from the other horses.

"Are you ready to go?" Father asks.

"Are you really going to let me go with you this time?" I ask in disbelief. Every morning my father makes his rounds to check on the fields and meets with the overseers. I am never allowed to go. My father always says I am too young. My mother never wants me to go because she doesn't trust the slaves and doesn't think a proper lady should be out and about in the fields. I don't care, I never want to be a proper lady. I would rather be outside exploring the creeks and woods with Benjamin than getting all dressed up and sipping tea at a boring party. The only thing that makes going to parties halfway fun is getting to see my best friend Mary, who lives on an adjacent farm. She is so much fun to be around. In fact, my mother said it was okay for her to come over later to have afternoon tea together. I look around, hardly able to contain my excitement. *This is going to be the best day ever,* I think while bouncing up and down.

My father and I make our way out to the fields. I can already tell it is going to be another hot, muggy August day. The sun shines bright against the morning dew and there is no trace of a cloud in the sky. We pass rows and rows of corn that will soon be harvested and make our way around to the tobacco fields. We grow the best tobacco in Kentucky, burley tobacco, and it is time to cut and hang it in the barns. The slaves have been working hard since dawn and have a few rows cut already. Children as young as me are working in the fields, sweating and already tired from the day. A wave of sadness overcomes me as I watch them work. *What if I had to work in the hot fields all day with no time to play and rest?* My sad thoughts are interrupted by a gruff voice and the light sound of horse hooves hitting the dirt.

"Good morning, sir and little lady," Lewis, our overseer says as he tips his hat to me. I like Lewis a great deal. He has been father's overseer since before I was born. He is quite scary looking though, with a big scar that extends from his eyebrow down into his beard. He also has long greasy brown hair that peeks out from his hat and goes all the way to his shoulders, but he has always been very kind to me, often bringing my brother and me sweet treats after his trips to town. I asked him once how he got his scary scar. He told me it was from a misunderstanding. I didn't know what that meant, so I asked

John. John told me it was because Lewis likes the ladies too much and went after the wrong one. I still didn't understand, but I let it go. I like him and that's all that matters to me.

"Good morning," I respond smiling.

"That's a very nice horse and a beautiful riding habit you have there, little lady."

"Thank you, it's my birthday."

"Well, happy birthday," he says as he hands me a small bouquet of wildflowers that he had picked on his way to the farm.

I take them beaming, "Thank you."

My father and Lewis converse for a few minutes and I go back to watching the slaves work in the field. This is the first time that I have actually watched them up close. I can see them from the upstairs window and hear their sad songs as they work, but I have never been allowed to go into the fields and be this close to them.

A loud crack wakes me from my reverie. I look up to see Lewis riding out to one of the women who is on her knees picking up a tobacco plant from the ground, cracking his whip as he goes. The woman's eyes grow wide and she puts her hands up to shield her face as Lewis starts beating her with a club. I can hear her pleading with Lewis and crying out in pain.

My father grabs Shadow's reins and tugs. "Let's go!" he orders.

"What happened? Why is he mad at her? What did she do?" I ask with tears in my eyes.

"She dropped the tobacco and may have damaged some of the leaves on the plant," my father explains.

"I don't understand. Please help her Daddy. It was only a

couple of plants and she is so small and they are so big and heavy. I drop things all the time but no one beats me with a stick. Please stop him from beating her," I whimper.

"Those plants are money. If they are damaged, they will not bring in as much money. We need money to live."

"But it was just a couple of plants!" I scream in between sobs.

"Young lady!" Father's voice booms. "Don't you ever raise your voice to me again. This is our way of life. This is how I provide for you, your brother, and your mother. I will not have you telling me how to treat my slaves. We are finished here. Take Shadow back to the stable and tell Benjamin to take care of her."

"Yes Father," I choke out in between sobs.

This is the first-time my father has spoken so harshly to me. My birthday is quickly turning into an unhappy day. I love my mother and father, but I don't always understand them.

I ride Shadow back to the stables as quickly as I can.

"How did she ride?" Benjamin asks with a smile that quickly fades as he catches sight of the tear stains on my face. "Josephine, what happened? Are you ok?"

"Boy, calling a white person by their name is one way to get yo' hide ripped off yo' back," Tom, the negro that has been taking care of our horses since before my family bought this farm, warns.

"You ain't gonna whip me, are you Jo?"

"No! I would never do that, you're my best friend."

Old Tom laughs, "You young'uns are gonna have to figure it out sooner than later. This here," he said pointing back and forth between Benjamin and I, "it ain't gonna happen."

I look at him bewildered and then I look at Benjamin. He nods his head and lowers his eyes to the floor.

"I don't understand," I say shaking my head.

"Don't understand little missy, or don't want too? You learn to accept this truth one day and when you do, you gonna be happy your skin be white."

What is going on? This world, which I always thought of as safe and happy, is turning uglier by the minute.

"I don't understand what any of this means," I cry as I turn and bolt out the door. I have to find John. I search around and finally find him at the creek fishing. I stumble upon him just as he is casting his line. I watch the bobber arc over the water and then settle on the surface with a plop.

"There's the birthday girl! I thought you would still be riding Shadow around the farm," he greets with a smile.

"John, it was horrible," I pout, immediately starting to cry again.

"What happened?" he asks as he drops his pole and runs to me.

I tell him the whole story, including what Old Tom had said.

"I don't understand why Benjamin and I can't be friends. I don't understand why we own negroes and why our mother and father are always telling us to treat others with respect, but we don't treat the negroes with respect. I don't understand," I whaled.

"Okay, okay, slow down. You and Benjamin are getting older; therefore, you won't be allowed to be friends, because he is black and you are white. When I was little, I used to play with Samuel, but then he went to work in the fields, so our friendship had to end. That's just the way it is."

"What does the color of our skin have to do with it? That is what I don't understand."

"Those with dark skin are ignorant. They don't know

anything and it is our job to take care of them."

"How can you say that? I feel that Benjamin is every bit as smart as you and me."

"Maybe with some things like taking care of horses, but he could never learn to read or write. Listen Jo, this is just the way things are. We own slaves. You own a slave. I don't know about you, but I like living how we live."

"You wouldn't if you were a slave and got a beating for the tiniest of things," I say as I turn and walk away angrily.

I was still fuming when Mary came to visit. We have lemonade instead of tea because it's so hot. I sip it slowly as Mary and I chat and I slowly feel myself relaxing and enjoying myself again. *This life I am living is a good one,* I tell myself. *I have Mary as a friend and she is just a field away. Even if I have to give up Benjamin, I will always have my Mary. Maybe this way of life isn't so bad.*

Chapter 9

The next few weeks go by as normal. I don't bring up what happened in the field and neither does my father. I think about it constantly, though, and come to the conclusion that I will never understand such harsh treatment for what seemed to me to be an accident.

It is midmorning on another hot and muggy summer day. My clothes are already sticking to me and I am just making my way out to the stable to discuss matters with Shadow. We often have long, serious talks. She is a good listener, especially when I have treats. I always love the way her muzzle feels so soft against my hands as she nibbles treats from them. I grab some hay, "Good morning, Shadow. I need to talk. My Aunt Diane is coming to teach me and my brother. For one thing, I don't like the thought of starting lessons again and another, I'm not sure about my aunt either. She lives in Delaware, is my father's sister, and I have never met her before. What if she is mean? You know, I really liked the teacher we had last year, but she went and got married and her husband doesn't want her to teach anymore. That's why I'm never getting married. I want to be able to come and go as I please and do what I want to do."

"I have been looking all over for you little missy," Millie

interjects as she bursts into the barn out of breath. "Your mother say she gonna whup me if I don't find you soon. She say she be needing you to go get your brother cuz she just received a letter from your aunt and she gonna be here today instead of tomorrow and he needs to travel into Maysville with the buggy and pick her up."

My stomach instantly turns into knots. John is down at slave row with my father at the holding pen. The thought of going to get him fills me with dread, not only because of what I saw firsthand a few weeks ago, but because there is a shipment of slaves that just came in. They will be taken to the sale in Washington tomorrow. The owner is afraid that if he continues on today that the slaves will be worn out and too sickly looking for tomorrow's sale to bring in maximum dollar. He thought it best that he stops and rests them here for a while and continues on in the morning. My father has a place to keep the slaves out back by slave row, but I have never been in there. I do not want to see the slaves up close. It was bad enough seeing their depressed and worn bodies as they walked the road back towards the holding pen, but seeing their faces up close, I fear, will be too much for me to handle. Sometimes I feel I was born into the wrong family. *Why can't I just be happy and accept this way of life as my brother has?*

I mount Shadow and we trot towards the holding pen. Mother would scold me for riding bareback again. She always tells me that a proper lady never rides without a saddle and never straddles a horse. Here I am breaking both rules and it is exhilarating. It always feels good to be free of my mother's scrutiny and her incessant desire to make me a proper southern young lady and just let myself go and laugh and play. My happy thoughts quickly shift as I arrive at the holding pen. As I hop down from Shadow, I can hear men shouting back and forth and the clanking of chains as men, women, and children shuffle into the holding pen. Depression and fear are etched on their faces. Children are crying, boys and girls no older or bigger than me. I look away from them and scan the area for John, hoping to find him quickly. I think I hear his voice inside the holding pen and head for it in desperation. I walk in and the smell of sweat and musk instantly fills my nose. I put my hand against the rough wall to steady myself until my eyes adjust to the dark room. I look around and I see some of the slaves being ushered upstairs, and with each step I can see large open sores on their legs where the shackles have been rubbing, red and raw. The sight is horrendous. A white man bumps into me as he drags a black man in and wrestles him to the ground, fastening his shackles to a metal ring on the ground.

"Try and get away now," the white man laughs. He turns and tips his hat to me, "My lady." I shiver and fight back tears. A feeling of hopelessness and despair overwhelms me.

"Josephine, what are you doing in here? You shouldn't be here." John asks worriedly. He grabs my hand and pulls me outside.

"Momma sent me for you. She said that Aunt Diane is going to be arriving in Maysville today instead of tomorrow. She needs you to head out straight away to meet her when her boat arrives."

"There he goes, catch him!" We hear a man yell. "He's running across the corn field towards the woods!"

We both look up to see a negro man running as fast as he can across the newly chopped corn field.

"I've got him!" shouts the slave owner's son as he takes off running after him.

He starts to catch up to the slave, who is still attached to his chains, but then he trips over a corn stalk and falls face first. He doesn't move. I can see the bloody corn stalk sticking out of the back of his head and I want to force myself to turn away from the sight, but no matter how much I want to, I can't. I feel John run past me, joining the chase, but I still can't move, rooted to the spot, heart pounding. I will the negro to run. I don't know what will happen to him if they catch him, but I know it probably won't be good. I hear shouting in the woods from the white men and mumbles from the slaves still held in captivity. Some of the slaves curse the runaway's stupidity while others pray for his safety.

I join the latter. Praying for the negro's safety goes against everything my family has taught me and lives for, but I can't help it. I can't stand to see him beat like the woman who dropped the tobacco plants. I see the men coming back and my heart sinks. I can see the slave being dragged behind a horse. His face is already bloodied and swollen from being beaten and dragged on his belly through the woods and across the field. The posse reaches the holding pen and the slave owner dismounts from his horse.

"This negro caused the death of my only son!" he roars as tears stream from his furious eyes and spit flies from his mouth. "Let this be an example to all you negroes who want to try and run away!" He viciously begins to whip the man, ripping shreds of skin from his back. The slave cries out in pain.

I bury my face in Shadow's side. I want to run and hide and pretend this isn't happening, but my feet refuse to move. Then, after what seems like an eternity, the whipping stops. I peer around Shadow and I catch sight of the negro taking shallow breaths. His back is ripped to shreds. There is not a piece of skin left, just raw muscle and blood dripping onto the dirt around him. With tears streaming down my face, I watch as they put a noose around his neck and drag him inside the holding pen. Everyone who isn't already chained up inside is made to follow. I wait until everyone is inside and then with wobbly legs creep up to the nearest window. I need to see what they are going to do to him. One of the white men tosses a rope over the nearest beam and hoists him into the air. The negro man's body jerks as his feet leave the ground. The man ties the rope off and leaves the man there, hanging, to die.

"Anyone even thinking about running away, you just remember this," one of the scraggly looking men spits as he begins to fasten their shackles to the metal rings.

"Josephine?" I hear my brother say. "Why are you still here?"

I turn away from the window with tears still streaming from my eyes. "I couldn't leave John, I just couldn't. Why? Why did that have to happen?" I sob.

John pulls me in and wraps his arms around me. "You shouldn't have stayed Jo. You shouldn't have stayed. Come on, let's get you back to the house."

He guides me up onto Shadow just as my father walks out of the slave pen.

"John, what is she doing here?" my father asks worriedly.

"It's okay Father, I've got her. I'll take her back to the house."

John guides me and Shadow back to the stable. I keep my head buried in her mane, not wanting to see anything or anyone.

I stay in my room the rest of the day. Every time I close my eyes, I see the negro, body jerking, hanging from the beam. Millie comes into my room towards evening and tells me that mother says I am supposed to get washed up for supper, my brother will be arriving soon with my aunt. I have no desire to eat, let alone meet my aunt. I had never seen a dead person before, but today I saw two. It is almost more than I can handle, but I do as I am told. I let Millie brush my hair, too numb to cry out when she pulls too hard, which I think upsets her because she starts to pull even harder. I don't understand why she wants to hurt me. I have always tried to treat her kindly, but I guess if I had been separated from my mother and father and forced to be a slave, I would be mad at everyone too.

By the time I make my way downstairs, my aunt has already arrived. She is seated at the table in a very plain brown dress. Her auburn hair is pulled back into a bun and she is wearing round, wire glasses. She looks as if she could be very cross. She and my father appear to be in a deep conversation that immediately ends when I enter the room.

"You must be Josephine," my aunt says as she walks towards me and embraces me in a tight hug. "It is so lovely to finally meet you. Your father is always talking about you and John in his letters. He has described you perfectly, right down to your auburn hair and brown eyes. She does look like me when I was younger, Edward."

"She's beginning to act like you too. She has quite a stubborn streak."

"Some may call it stubborn, but I call it strong-willed and confident," she corrects with a wink.

I smile. I think I'm going to like my aunt.

After supper, I retreat back to my room. I attempt to sleep, but fail miserably. I can't get the images of the dead slave out of my head. I get up and take Benjamin's doll out of its hiding spot in the closet and hold it tightly. I'm still hugging it when

I hear a light knock on my bedroom door. I quickly hide the doll under my pillow. The moon let in just enough light for me to see to cross the room. I open the door to find my aunt standing in her night clothes.

"May I come in?" she asks.

I open the door wider for her to enter. She motions me over to the bed and we sit down.

"I hope I didn't wake you."

"No," I say shaking my head. "I can't seem to get any sleep tonight."

"That's understandable after what you witnessed today. Would you like to talk about it?"

I take a deep breath, unsure if I should open up to her. She places her arm around me and hugs me tightly.

"It's ok," she assures me, "you can tell me anything."

I start slow, but once the tears start falling, I spill everything. I tell her how awful my experience was today and how nobody seemed to care anything about the slave. I tell her how I don't understand how my family can go to church on Sundays, listen to the preacher preach about Jesus and love, yet turn around and own another human being and treat them so cruel at times. I tell her I don't think it is fair that my friend Benjamin and I probably aren't going to be allowed to be friends anymore, because we are growing up and it isn't proper for a white woman to be friends with a black man. All of my thoughts, worries, and concerns tumble out of me and onto her. She listens quietly until I finish with everything I have to say and waits patiently until I regain control of myself.

"You are so very much like me," she says smiling and wiping away a tear from my cheek. "I am so sorry you had to see that gruesome event today. I wish I could tell you that it has only happened once, but I cannot. Events like you witnessed today happen all over the south every single day. The negro people are enslaved just because they have a different color skin. They are sold away from their families, forced to work long hours in hot fields, beaten, raped, and often even killed as you saw today. I know you are young and may not know what some of what I just said is exactly, but it is good for you to know the true evils of slavery. I am glad to see that you have a mind and heart of your own and that you can see the negroes as what they are, people. I had to leave the south and move up north in order to get away from the cruelties of slavery that I grew up with."

"But isn't Delaware a slave state?" I ask.

"Ah, yes. Delaware is a slave state. I didn't move directly from Kentucky to Delaware. My initial move was to Philadelphia. I moved there not only to escape living with slavery, but also for a good, solid education. I attended the Young Ladies' Academy and learned a great deal, which is how I am able to teach you and John this year. I met some wonderful people in Philadelphia, many who have similar thoughts about slavery. It was this group of people that directed me to make my move to Delaware to teach children and to seek out others who had the same feelings about slavery as we did. We were hoping that if we were able to gather enough people, we could entice the state of Delaware to abolish slavery; however, once I received Edward's letter asking me if I could come teach my niece and nephew, I knew God was telling me that my work in Delaware was over and it was time to return home to take on an even greater challenge."

"Is teaching me and John really going to be that challenging, Aunt Diane?"

"Oh, no, sweetheart. Teaching you two will be a pleasure. My challenge is of a different sort. Although you appear to be much older than your age, I will have to wait to discuss this with you until I feel you are ready to take on such a responsibility. Do you think you can get some sleep now? We have a big day ahead of us tomorrow."

"Yes, I think so. Thank you for listening. I can't seem to get anyone here to listen to me. John is always so good at explaining things and talking to me, but when it comes to my concerns of slavery, he doesn't understand how or why I think the way I do. He just says that he likes our way of life."

"Slavery for most in the south is a way of life. There are few who live here that see slavery as the evil that it is, but if they do, they are like John and dismiss it because they enjoy the privileged lives they are allowed to live because of it. You have your own beautiful mind, Josephine, and you see the true evils of slavery. Together we can make a difference, but right now we both need to get our rest. Sweet dreams, Jo."

"Good night, Aunt Diane."

I smile happily in the dark, thankful that I found someone that I can confide in.

Chapter 10

I wake up to the rumble of thunder. I feel as dark and dreary as the sky, tired from staying up late last night. Millie comes in grumpy as ever and helps me get dressed and fixes my hair. I try to make polite conversation, but she just grunts at my questions. Today is wash day, and she hates wash day.

"At least it won't be too hot for you when you are doing the wash today," I offer trying to bring something positive to her day.

"It don't matter, it still gonna tear the skin off my hands. Make them all raw so no boy gonna want to hold my hand."

I blush at the thought of a boy holding my hand. "You are pretty, Millie, you have the most beautiful brown eyes and golden-brown skin. Any boy would love to hold your hand," I compliment shyly.

"Beautiful brown skin, you say? It's this brown skin that make me your slave," she snaps back harshly.

Mother would be appalled that I let Millie talk back to me that way, but I didn't have the heart to scold her.

"I'm sorry, Millie, truly I am."

"If you really sorry, you set me free," she says as she grabs my wash and leaves the room.

I am dumbfounded. I had never thought to set Millie free,

but after all, she is my property and I can do with her what I want. *I am no different from my family.* Sadly, I did enjoy the way that I lived at the expense of the slaves. *Maybe I should just learn to live with it and go about my life. After all, it is easier to conform.*

I make my way down to breakfast where I am met by my aunt and the rest of the family. Thunder cracks and I jump, making everyone laugh. We have a delicious breakfast of eggs, grits, and biscuits with the creamiest gravy, but what Millie said about me setting her free weighs so heavily on my mind that I can barely taste it.

"Father," I say rather unsure.

"Yes, dear?"

"Can I set Millie free?"

My mother drops her fork with a loud clank and stares at me astounded.

"Why would you want to do that, sweetheart?" my father asks patiently.

"Because I don't like owning her. She is mean to me."

"You have to learn to control your slave, young lady. I have told you this before," my mother replies curtly.

"She will learn, Charlotte, it will just take time. To answer your question, Jo, you are too young to buy, sell, or set free any slave without my signature and I will not sign off on setting Millie free at this time. You must, as your mother said, learn to control your slave so she will be more obedient."

"Yes, Father," I reply meekly.

After breakfast, my father heads out to check on the fields and my mother goes to oversee that the wash and other household chores are being performed properly while Aunt Diane, John, and I set up in the study for our first day of class. I feel excited and ready to learn from our aunt, but John isn't too thrilled. He would rather be out in the fields with father. The morning session flies by and before I know it, it's time for lunch. The rain has stopped and the day is turning into a beautiful one. Aunt Diane asks Frannie to make some sandwiches so we can have a picnic lunch outside. Benjamin comes out of the stables just as we are finishing up our lunch. I stand up and wave to him and he smiles and waves in return.

"Is that your friend Benjamin?" Diane asks.

"Yes."

She rises and calls him over.

"Yes ma'am?" Benjamin stammers, averting his eyes from her.

"I'm Diane," she introduces extending her hand. "Josephine and John's aunt. It's nice to meet you."

Benjamin looks around quickly, then he slowly takes my aunt's hand and shakes it, keeping his eyes on the ground.

"It's okay, young man, you can look me in the eyes."

Benjamin looks at my aunt and smiles, "It's nice to meet you too, ma'am."

"I was just about to give John and Josephine a brief recess. If you aren't busy and want to play with them, that is fine with me."

His eyes light up. "Yes ma'am, thank you ma'am."

Benjamin and I immediately start a game of chase and John eventually joins in after a little bit of coaxing. Even my aunt joins in for a while. We play until we are all out of breath and laughing, then it is time to go in for our afternoon session. I say goodbye to Benjamin and we part ways. I go back to classes while Benjamin heads to the stable to get the horses ready to take my father to a nearby farm so he can discuss a business transaction.

The afternoon session is over just as quickly as the morning session and soon we are back together as a family, eating dinner, and discussing our day. Mother is happy because all the wash was finished and my father says his business transaction went over amicably. We are now owners of two more horses that he felt, if handled correctly, could be prize winners in future horse races. John surprisingly says he did enjoy his first day of school even though he would have liked to have been helping with the business transaction. And, of course, Aunt Diane and I had a great day as well.

After supper, we take a stroll down an old dirt path that passes under a tunnel of trees and out into a meadow where several horses are grazing. We feed the horses treats as the grown-ups talk and John and I explore the area, catching grasshoppers and other creatures. As the sun starts to set, the sky turns the most beautiful shade of pink and orange and we make our way back to the porch where Frannie has ice, cold lemonade waiting for us. As I sit on the porch drinking my lemonade, I thank God for this beautiful day, hoping he will bring many more.

The next few weeks run along in much the same way, except the days are getting shorter and chillier. I am in the stable telling Shadow all about my day when I hear a noise. I stop to listen.

"Boo!" Benjamin shouts as he grabs me from behind.

I scream loudly and turn around quickly, eyes wide and heart racing.

"That's not funny," I say while throwing a handful of straw at him. He ducks out of the way laughing. "You really scared me this time."

"Sorry, I couldn't resist," he says still laughing. "You should have seen your face."

I can't help but laugh along with him. I bet I did look funny.

"What did you do today?" Benjamin asks curiously.

"Aunt Diane took us outside and we learned all about how and why leaves change color."

"Wow, learning sounds fun."

"It's not always fun. Sometimes it gets a bit boring."

"What is so boring?"

"Well, we have to learn how to read and write."

"What is that? Is it hard?"

"Reading and writing? Well, I don't really know how to explain it to you other than it's putting letters together, making words, writing them down, and reading them out loud. Sometimes it's hard when the words are really big."

"What are letters?"

"Here, let me show you." I grab a stick and write out the A, B, C's making sure to go over what sound each letter makes as I go.

Benjamin catches on quickly and before I know it, he is spelling small words like cat and dog.

"If you want, since you aren't allowed to join me in classes, we can have our own classes here and I will teach you in the evenings."

"That sounds fun! Do you think it's okay, though? Old Tom says we colored folk aren't allowed to learn to read and write. It'd get us whipped. Is that true?"

"I won't tell if you won't tell. Besides, nobody should care, they don't think you can learn anyway."

"Josephine! It's time to come in now, it's getting late!"

"Mother is calling, I better go. Goodnight, Benjamin."

"Goodnight, Jo."

Months go by and Christmas comes and goes. Spring is quickly approaching and it will soon be planting time again. School is winding down and although part of me likes the thought of not having to sit and learn all day, Aunt Diane has made it fun and exciting. I continue to teach Benjamin every evening and he is learning very quickly. He is definitely catching on to math quicker than I am and can read the same books that I can.

We hunker down a little further in the straw in the stable on this chilly March evening, Benjamin and I are happily discussing a book we have just read together when the stable door opens letting in a big gust of wind. Benjamin quickly stands up and starts nervously tending to the nearest horse.

"What ya'll be doing in here every evening?" Millie asks haughtily as she closes the door behind her.

"I come here to do my studies and visit with Shadow," I reply without hesitation.

"It seem to me like I walk past here and hear you teachin' Benjamin all 'bout readin' and writin'. You be teachin' him 'bout dat stuff Missy Josephine?"

"It's of no concern of yours, Millie, what I am doing in the stable. Why don't you go back to the house?"

Millie seems taken back by my boldness to tell her what to do, since I have never spoken to her like that before, but she remains stone-faced.

"Actually, little Missy, it is, cause what if I's go on up to da house and tells your momma dat you teachin' Benjamin here how to read and write. What do you think she would say bout dat?"

"You wouldn't dare do something like that," I say as I stand up to confront her.

"Please, Millie, don't tell on me. I just want to learn and be smart like white folk," Benjamin pleads.

"I's gonna keep this a secret for you, Benjamin, if your little friend here teach me too," she promises slyly.

I pause not knowing what to do. I don't want to teach Millie. Not because I don't think she can learn, but because I enjoy my evenings with Benjamin in the stable. We study, play, and discuss our day. I don't want Millie to get in the way of that happiness with her hatefulness. I am also afraid that she will brag to other slaves in the house that I am teaching her and not them. The last thing I need is for all of the slaves to be coming to me to learn to read and write, or worse for my mother or father to find out that I am teaching them.

"I'd rather not teach you, Millie."

"Suit yourself, I's gonna go back to da house then."

Benjamin grabs my arm in panic. "What if she tells? I'm gonna get whipped!"

"I won't let that happen to you."

"Were you able to stop that woman from being whipped in the field that day?"

Benjamin is right, nobody listens to me. If my father finds out Benjamin can read and write, he will whip him for sure whether I plead with him or not.

I run out of the stable after Millie as fast as my legs can carry me. I catch up to her just as she is entering the garden that leads to the back entrance of the house.

"Millie," I wheeze, trying to catch my breath. I see my mother out on her evening stroll around the house, making sure everything is in order. "Do you want to come play with me in the stable?" I ask, trying to contain my annoyance so as not to raise suspicion from my mother.

She smiles slyly, "Yes, that would be fun."

Teaching Millie is not fun. She is not learning nearly as quickly as Benjamin, so I have to spend most of my time going over the alphabet and simple words with her when I really want to spend it with Benjamin. Tom is never around during our studies. He doesn't want any part of it because once we are found out, and he said that day will come, he wants to be safe from the whip. No one seems to be suspicious, except for maybe Aunt Diane. Every time I head out to the stable in the evenings, she always tells me to be careful. I'm not sure if she is afraid that I will get kicked by a horse or if she really knows what I am doing. If she knows, she never tries to stop me.

Chapter 11

Summer has come to Kentucky in full force. It hasn't rained for a full week! The crops are beginning to wilt out in the fields and everyone is irritable and cranky. Benjamin and I decide to move our study session this evening down by the creek. The shade from all the trees is welcoming and the water is cool on our toes as we let our feet dangle in the creek. I have to keep moving my toes because a pesky crawdad keeps trying to pinch them. Benjamin and I start discussing our day and the heat as we wait for Millie to arrive. She walks up to us and is cranky as ever, fussing about this and that. We don't even know what she is going on about, so we ignore her and go back to our conversation. This must have really made her mad, because the next thing we know a rock comes flying past our heads. It barely misses the both of us. We look up angrily.

"What was that for?" Benjamin asks. "You could have hit one of us."

"Good, then maybe you will listen!" she screams.

"How about we just get started?" I suggest sternly.

I start Millie off on writing the alphabet in the dirt. It's been months and she is still trying to figure out the alphabet. I don't even know why she still comes other than to make my life miserable. I sit back down next to Benjamin and begin reading Oliver Twist out loud while he continues working on the portraits that he is drawing of the two of us. The drawings look so much like us, it is amazing. He just finishes and rips the paper in half, giving me his portrait, while he keeps mine when something stings my arm. I look down to find a stick lying beside me. I jump up and glare at Millie, "What is wrong with you?"

"You are supposed to be teaching me, but you spend more time paying attention to Benjamin."

"You have some nerve, Millie. Don't you know I could have you whipped for striking me with that stick? I have half a nerve to do it myself."

"Hit me and I'll tell that Benjamin knows how to read and write."

"I won't hit you Millie, that is not who I am, but I'm not going to teach you anymore so please go back to the house and don't bother me about this again. I don't want to see you right now."

Surprisingly, Millie does as she is told. I sit back down with Benjamin. He rubs my arm where a welt has formed. "Are you okay?"

"Yes, thank you. I don't understand her. I try to be nice to her and she is nothing but mean to me."

"She has had a rough life. She was sold away from her mother and father to be your slave. She will most likely never see them again. I couldn't imagine never seeing my mother again. It would break my heart."

"I understand. How come you aren't mean and hateful like her, though? You are a slave too."

"I got lucky. I never knew my father, but I still have my momma with me. I also like working with the horses, and I have you, Jo. You're my best friend. I'd rather talk to you than any of the boys on slave row." He turns and looks me square in the eye with a serious face. "Josephine, I don't know what will happen to me when I am older, if I'll be sold away or what, but always remember that no matter where I am, I will always be thinking of my best friend and I will do my best to find my way back to you again."

I didn't know what to say. I didn't want to think any further than us being here now, having fun as children. I didn't want to think about the possibility of us being torn apart as adults. Tears came to my eyes as I hug him tightly, not caring one bit who sees me.

"I will do my best to keep you safe and never let anything bad happen to you. I will always try to keep you and your momma together and I will go to the ends of the world looking for you. You're my best friend too."

"What are you doing down here with that boy, young lady!"

I jump. I turn to see my mother looking furious. "I...I'm not doing anything mother, just sitting here talking to Benjamin."

"Look at you, looking like a little heathen. No better than a negro child with your bare feet in the creek and your dress pulled up to your knees. My mother would be appalled at the way you are behaving and worse yet, Millie came and told me some very disturbing news and by the looks of that book there, it must be the truth."

"I was just sitting here reading Oliver Twist to Benjamin."

"Were you reading it to him or was he reading it with you? Did you teach that boy to read and write?"

I don't know what to say. My heart is pounding. I don't want to lie to mother, but I don't want Benjamin to get into trouble either.

"No mother, he can't read and write, he's just a dumb negro boy," I manage to stammer.

"Don't you lie to me, young lady."

"Boy," she opens the book to a page and hands it to Benjamin. "Read this page."

Benjamin takes the book shaking, clearly not knowing what to do either. He looks from me to my mother with terror in his eyes.

"I can't read, ma'am."

Smack! Pain sears across my cheek and my eyes start to water. It takes me a minute to comprehend that my mother just hit me. She has never laid a hand on me before. I have only seen her hit Millie and other house slaves.

"Why did you hit me?" I demand, voice quivering.

"If you're going to act like a dumb, dirty negro, I'm going to treat you like one. You both are lying to me. Boy, if you don't show me you can read that book, I'm going to beat Josephine right in front of you."

I can't believe it. Mother is threatening to beat me, her own daughter, because I taught Benjamin how to read and write. Many emotions are running through my mind, sadness and fear among them, but then I see Millie out of the corner of my eye smiling at the scene before her and then only anger courses through my veins.

"Ma'am," Benjamin begs, "Please don't hurt Josephine. I can read and write. Please don't hit Josephine anymore. I'll take the beating, just don't hurt her. Please, ma'am."

"You'd take a beating for Josephine?"

"Yes ma'am, I don't wanna see her get hurt."

"Well you're in luck, because I don't think I will beat anyone tonight. My hand stings already and I don't wish to cause myself any more pain this evening. Josephine has done enough of that already through her lies and deceit. Don't think you are getting let off the hook though, your punishment will come tomorrow. I just don't know in what form yet. Let's go, Josephine."

Benjamin and I exchange worried looks and then I turn and follow my mother back to the house, anger still coursing through my veins as Millie walks ahead.

Once back at the house I go straight up to my room. I am so mad at Millie I can barely even see straight. How could she be so mean? I understand how she could tell on me, but not Benjamin. He is a slave just like her. Millie must know I am upset with her, because she hasn't come up to my room to help me get ready for bed. It doesn't matter, I can do it on my own anyway. I am very thirsty, so after I wriggle into my night gown, I put my night cap on and tiptoe out into the hallway. I make it halfway down the stairs when I hear voices in the study. It is my mother and father arguing. I come to a halt and listen intently.

"I think we should sell him."

"We will not sell him; he knows the horses. He is young but much better at handling them than Tom ever was."

"He knows how to read and write, Edward. A slave that can read and write is always trouble. No telling what else Josephine has been teaching him. She has an infatuation with him and he with her, and we must end it now!"

"She is just a little girl, Charlotte. She lives out here on this farm with only Mary close by to play with. Benjamin is her age and they like to play together. There is no harm in that at the moment. As far as knowing how to read and write, give him a few days and he will forget how."

"I want you to sell that boy, Edward!"

"Charlotte, I will not sell him, Tom won't be fit to drive in another year or so. He is already having trouble seeing. We need a driver if you expect to continue going to your parties."

"We can find another driver at the next slave auction. Sell that boy, Edward!"

"I will not!"

There was silence for a moment. I couldn't believe what I was hearing. My mother was trying to sell my best friend.

"I'll tell you what, Charlotte. If it makes you feel any better, I will send him down to slave row and have him work in the fields until Tom is no longer useful."

"Sell him, Edward, I'm begging you, he is no good."

"He will go to slave row and work in the fields and that is final."

At the sound of foot-steps I quickly turn and dash up the stairs and back to my room throwing myself on the bed and pounding my fists in anger. *This can't be happening. They are sending Benjamin to slave row and it's all my fault. He'll have to work long, hard hours in the hot sun tending to the crops and possibly meeting with the overseer's whip. I won't get to see his smiling face every day. I should have never taught him to read and write. What was I thinking? At least my father isn't going to sell him, at least he will still be close by.* I rush to my closet, grab the corn husk doll, and hold it tightly wishing this was all just a dream.

I climb out of bed, body sore from being so tense most of the night. Millie comes in to help me dress, looking quite smug. I don't greet her with my usual good morning, but she doesn't seem to care. She starts going about her usual routine and even begins humming.

"What are you so happy about today?" I ask grumpily.

"I's just in a good mood today, that's all," she says with a little smile.

"Is it because you got me and Benjamin in trouble and got him sent down to slave row to work in the fields?"

"I hate dat 'bout Benjamin being sent to work in da fields, but it sure was good to see you get slapped."

I'm shocked. "Why would you enjoy that? Why are you so mean to me?"

"You the reason I got sold from my momma. I ain't never gonna like you."

"I'm very sorry that happened to you, Millie, truly I am, but I didn't have anything to do with it. I was young when my father bought you for me."

"You's can set me free though, you own me."

"I can't Millie, I am too young to make that decision. You are both mine and my father's property and I cannot set you free without his consent. He would never allow me to set you free right now. Trust me, Millie, when I am old enough, I will set you free. I don't like you any more than you like me. I've tried my hardest to be kind to you, but you make it really difficult for me," I say as I leave the room.

I make my way to the study for my lessons with John and Aunt Diane. The day is turning out to be humid. I can't concentrate on my studies, constantly thinking about Benjamin in the hot fields. *Maybe it was all a dream,* I think wishfully.

As soon as we get a break for lunch I rush upstairs to look out upon the fields, searching for Benjamin. There are dark bodies everywhere, bending over the earth and planting tiny tobacco plants. The overseer cracks his whip overhead to make sure the slaves don't slow their pace or injure the plants. I don't see him. A wave of relief sweeps over me, but then the overseer steers his horse out of the way and I spy Benjamin stooped over, sweat glistening off his back.

"No!" I yell.

"Young ladies don't scream like that. What is wrong with you?" Mother scolds as she walks into the room.

"Why is Benjamin in the field, Mother?" I ask, even though I know the answer.

"That is his punishment for you teaching him to read and write."

"He should not be punished this way; he should not be punished at all!" I scream at my mother in between sobs of anger and frustration.

Another blow hits me hard on the cheek. This is starting to become normal, my mother slapping me. I barely even feel it amid all of my other feelings.

"You will not talk to me like that again, do you understand me? Slaves are forbidden to learn to read and write. His punishment could have been much worse. I wanted to sell him off, but your father said no. I feel he is wrong and that boy is nothing but trouble for you, but I must obey your father's wishes."

"Benjamin is my friend."

"Benjamin is a negro, a slave! I should have put a stop to you and that boy associating years ago. Mary is just a farm away, go and play with her if you must. It is high time for you to stop that childish nonsense anyway and start to act like the woman that you are becoming."

"It's not just about playing with Benjamin. He is not used to working such long hours in the fields and I don't want him to get hurt."

"You have such a big heart, Josephine, but if you are going to be a good wife and slave owner, you must forget your childish ways and learn how to control you and your husband's slaves. Allowing them to manipulate you into teaching them to read and write shows you are weak and no man is going to want a weak wife. I feel I have done all I can with you, trying to raise you right to be a good, strong woman. I'm not sure where I failed you. I have been thinking about it and if your father won't let me sell that boy, then I think it is time for you to leave and live with my mother. She raised me to be a good, strong, God-fearing, slaveholding woman. Hopefully she can correct the mistakes that I made with you and teach you the ways of a true southern woman."

I can't believe what I am hearing, I am speechless. My mother is going to send me away, like a slave. My father often travels to Natchez, Mississippi, where my grandmother lives. He gathers up whatever slaves he wants to sell, marches them to Maysville, loads them on a boat, and sells them at auctions along the way. It was on one of these trips that my mother and father met. He eventually married my mother and brought her to live on this farm after he bought it.

"You are sending me off to Natchez like a slave?"

"No, sweetheart, I am sending you down to live with your grandmother for a while, so she can teach you how to be the true southern woman that you are. Since my brother has taken over the plantation, she will have the time to teach you; whereas, I have too much on my hands running my own household at the moment."

"Is Father okay with this?"

"I ran it past him this morning and he believes that it is a good idea as well. He and John are going to be taking a shipment of slaves down in a week's time and you will travel with them."

At that she turns and leaves me alone in the room. Tears form in my eyes as I turn and look out upon the field. I can still see Benjamin working hard. At least he isn't being sold further south. Maybe after I leave, he will be allowed to come back to the stable. I will have to talk to Father about it on our trip. I don't like the thought of leaving my home one bit, but if it will help Benjamin leave the tortuous fields, then I will gladly do it.

I sprint out across the hay field and down through the creek, not caring if my feet get wet. I run all the way to Mary's house. I make it all the way to the porch where Mary is sitting with her mother sipping on lemonade before I stop to catch my breath.

"Josephine, is everything okay?" her mother asks concernedly.

Mary's mother, Ruby, has always been quite a bit different from my mother. She seems kinder and I find I can talk to her better.

"My mother is sending me away to live with my grandmother in Natchez," I manage to get out.

"Are you happy or sad?"

"Of course she's sad, Mother. I'm sad. Jo, who am I going to talk to at the parties?"

"I don't know, Mary. I'm going to miss you so much."

"When are you leaving and how long are you going to be visiting your grandmother?" Ruby asks.

"I leave in a week when my father and John travel down with the slaves. I don't know how long I am staying. I guess until I become a good, strong, southern woman, according to my mother," I say as I roll my eyes.

"I don't want you to go, Jo! Why is she sending you away?"

I lower my eyes, not sure if I should tell them the reason. They will probably look at me like a traitor as well.

"It's okay Josephine, you don't have to tell us," Ruby states as she gives me a hug. "We will miss you a great deal and hope to see you back racing across our fields soon. You two go and play if you would like."

"Thank you," both Mary and I respond.

Mary and I walk down to the creek where I immediately take off my shoes and stockings and stick my feet in the water. Mary hesitates. I look at her questioningly.

"Mother says I need to be more ladylike now that I am getting older."

"Not you too. I am just about tired of all this talk about growing up and being a lady. If being all proper means I can't get dirty and play, then I don't want to grow up, ever."

Mary gasps. "Don't you want to grow up and find a beau?"

"Maybe one day, but not anytime soon. I only have a few more days left here and I want to enjoy myself."

Mary looks around before sliding her shoes and socks off and placing her feet in the water. "It does feel good. So, what did you do to make your mother send you away?"

"You will probably be mad at me too."

"No, I won't. You're my best friend, I couldn't be mad at you."

"If I tell you, please don't tell anyone else. I don't want everyone to know and think ill of me like my family seems to now."

"I won't tell a soul."

"I taught Benjamin how to read and write."

"You did what?" she replies in astonishment.

"Do you think I am a bad person?"

"No, I don't think you are a bad person. But why did you do it?"

"I don't know. Benjamin is my friend and when you aren't around, I talk to him. He is smart and interested in the same things as me. We were talking about my lessons and I asked if he wanted to learn too. He said yes and so I started to teach him."

"Could he learn?"

"Of course, he is no different than you and me, he just has a different color skin."

"You are a funny girl, Josephine."

"Why do you say that?"

"Because you care about all things. I have never met anyone else like you."

"Thank you, Mary. I'll take that as a compliment. You aren't mad at me or think I am a bad person?"

"Of course not, you are my best friend and I am going to miss you terribly."

We spend the rest of the afternoon relaxing and talking down by the creek.

"Mary, your momma say it's time for you to get washed up for supper. You invited to supper if you like, Josephine," Annette, Mary's slave says.

"Thank you, but I better go home. It is bad enough that I have missed afternoon lessons; missing supper too probably isn't a good idea, especially since I don't think anyone knows where I am." I hug Mary tightly and walk back home, consumed by somber thoughts.

My room is dark as I lay in bed. I hear a light tap on my

bedroom door. I tuck the cornhusk doll under my pillow and make my way to the door. I open it up to find my aunt Diane standing as she did on her first night here, in her night cap and gown.

"May I come in?"

I nod and we sit on the bed.

"I heard what happened. I just want to let you know that what you did, teaching Benjamin to read and write, was very brave. Although your mother doesn't think you are a strong woman, I do. You are very smart, compassionate, caring, and you're not afraid to follow your heart and do what you think is right even if it goes against the majority. To me, that is the true definition of strength. Your mother is a hard woman and I hear her mother is even more strict and cruel. You must stay true to your heart. Don't let them take away all the good you have inside. Although it may not seem like it, there are many people who have the same beliefs and think like you. They feel that the only difference between white people and negroes is the color of their skin. They feel colored people should have the same opportunities as white people and should no longer be enslaved and mistreated."

"Really?"

"Yes, and do you promise not to tell a soul what I am about to tell you? If you do, it can get me into a lot of trouble."

My heart is slamming against my chest. I have no idea what she is about to tell me. "I promise."

"I am one of those people, an abolitionist," she begins. "I am a part of an organization called the Pennsylvania Anti-Slavery Society. It is because of this organization that I ended up in Delaware as part of the Underground Railroad. I would aid escaped slaves on their travels through Delaware into

83

Pennsylvania."

My mouth drops, "You could get into a lot of trouble if anyone finds out.

"That is why, my dear, you must not tell a soul."

"I won't tell anyone. I don't want you to get into trouble, I love you.

"And I love you."

She hugs me tightly and we sit in silence for a moment.

"I don't want to go to Natchez. I've never been and I won't know anybody."

"I know you don't want to go. The reason they are making you go is absurd as well. You are never going to be a slave owner or act like one. You have too big a heart for that and too much respect for all people, regardless of color. I have learned, though, that things happen to us for a reason. There is a reason that you are going to Natchez."

"What is the reason?" I ask confusedly.

"I don't know. That is something you will have to figure out while you are down there. Pay attention to everything around you and use this experience to learn and grow. For example, what did you learn from teaching Benjamin to read and write?"

"I learned that I should not do it again."

"Is that what you learned?"

"Yes, because it got us into trouble. He is out in the fields and I am being sent away to Natchez."

"So, you think that Benjamin learning to read and write caused that change to happen?"

"Well, not really. Mother finding out caused everything to change."

"Did you enjoy teaching Benjamin?"

"Yes."

"Do you think that all children should have the opportunity to learn regardless of their color?"

"Yes."

"Okay, then do you think you should not teach Benjamin or someone like Benjamin again?"

I think for a moment. I really liked teaching and studying with Benjamin and I didn't want to stop. If I stayed here, I would still continue to teach him, wouldn't I?

"No, if I were staying here, I would still teach Benjamin. I would just be more careful and I would try to keep it a secret from everyone, but most definitely I would keep it from Millie, because she is only out for herself."

"You are learning quickly, Josephine. You will make a great abolitionist one day," she says, planting a kiss on the top of my head.

I smile sleepily.

"Goodnight and sweet dreams, Jo."

"Good night, aunty."

Chapter 12

The following days fly by. All of my pretty dresses and crinolines are packed away into trunks along with my everyday dresses. It is the night before our departure and time to say my goodbyes to everyone. I have been putting it off, ignoring the fact that I am leaving. I go to the stable first to give Shadow extra treats and hugs and tell Tom goodbye and to please take extra good care of Shadow while I am away. He says that he will do it just for his favorite little missy.

My next stop is the house slave quarters above the kitchen. I barely walk through the door when I am scooped up in a great big hug.

"Oh, little missy, I's gonna miss you so much. I baked ya a few cookies to take with ya on your travels."

I bite into one and it's so delicious and sweet on my tongue that before I know it, the whole thing has disappeared.

"Thank you, Frannie. I'm going to miss you too," I say while wiping the crumbs from my mouth.

She engulfs me in another big hug and I hold onto her tightly, trying to fight back tears.

"You make sure that cook down there feed you right, okay?" she commands between sobs.

"I will, Frannie."

I climb the stairs to look for the other house slaves. Benjamin's mother, Ann, is the one I really want to see. Once I find her, I immediately begin to apologize for the hundredth time for getting her son sent down to slave row.

"I'm going to miss you terribly, Ann, but maybe after I leave Benjamin will be able to come back here and live and work in the stable again."

"I hope so, but that will be the only good thing that comes from you leaving. My boy, Benjamin, isn't going to be the same with you gone. You all he talk about. I miss hearing him chatter about you before he drift off to sleep. Now both my babies are gonna be gone. I don't know what I'm gonna do with myself."

"Hopefully I won't be gone long. I'm going to go see Benjamin now. I can't leave without saying goodbye to my best friend."

"You be careful while you gone little missy, and come back home soon."

I give her a hug and leave quickly before either of us has a chance to cry.

I walk quickly along the dirt path down towards slave row. The sun has just set, turning the sky into a brilliant shade of orange with a hint of pink, but I know the light will fade quickly. I can see rain clouds coming. Mother would kill me if she knew where I was going. I wasn't allowed to go to slave row in the daytime, let alone in the dark. Mother says the darkies can't be trusted.

When I finally reach slave row my heart sinks. There are rows and rows of tiny cabins and I don't know which one Benjamin is living in. I scan the area searching for a familiar face. There are slaves everywhere. I walk up to one woman to ask her if she knows Benjamin and if she knows where he might be. Without looking at me, she says she knows him, but does not know where he is this evening. Disappointed, I walk further into slave row, hearing whispers behind me, slaves asking one another what the master's daughter is doing down on slave row.

"What brings you down here, little missy?"

I turn to see a scraggly looking slave walking towards me and looking me straight in the eyes. He is very thin, filthy, and I can smell his stink even though I am several feet away from him.

"Don't you go and do nothing ignorant and get yourself hung Ezekiel," another man cautions.

"Ignorant? That's what we is ain't it? Just dumb, ignorant slaves. Got no smarts and got no feelings. I have feelings, little missy, and I still have a lot of feelings that course through my veins when I think about the way those white men treated my Bessie. They the reason why she gone. Used her body for their own pleasure. Put her in her grave, little missy. I always told myself I'd get revenge on them white folk for what they did to her all those years ago and it looks like tonight is my night. They'll kill me for sure tomorrow, but seeing the life go out of you tonight and knowing that my Bessie is smiling down on me the whole time will be well worth facing the whip and the rope."

I don't know what to do. Ezekiel is moving closer and closer, his frenzied eyes never leaving mine. My mind is screaming run, but my feet are rooted to the ground.

"Don't you touch her!"

Benjamin appears and quickly steps in between me and Ezekiel. A sigh of relief escapes my lips.

"What do you think you are going to do, boy? You think you can stop me? Get out of the way or I'll kill you too."

Benjamin refuses to waver, standing his ground as the man towers over him.

"I will not let you hurt her. She never did anything to you. Please, just let her be. She is here to see me."

"She's white. That is reason enough for me to kill her. White folk bring nothing but pain and heartache to us all."

"She's different, she sees us as equals."

"She got you buffaloed, boy. Ain't no white person see a negro as an equal. They see us as their property. Here to do their dirty work and make them money. They rip our families apart, tearing babies from mother's arms, they use us and abuse us, then dispose of us when we are of no use to them. You young, boy, you don't know the pain they can cause like I do. You don't know how it feels to have someone you love taken from you by white folk! You haven't heard the woman you love screaming for you to help her as white men ravage her body, unable to help her because they have beaten you half senseless. All I wanted to do was marry that woman, to make her my own, but they took that from me! Now it's my turn to take something from them! Move, boy!"

He grabs Benjamin and tosses him to the side. I start to tremble and take a step back. Though the man is smiling, I can only see hate in his eyes. He reaches out for me, his sweaty hands grabbing hold of my arms. I scream and try to run, but it is too late. I can't move. Tears of pure fright form as I plead with him not to hurt me. Despite all the other slaves around, no one seems to want to help me.

CRACK! The lights go out in Ezekiel's eyes. His grip loosens and he falls to the ground with a thud. A woman holding what looks like a sturdy tree limb stands with Benjamin breathing heavily. I immediately recognize her as the same woman that was whipped by the overseer for dropping the tobacco on my birthday.

"Thank you," I manage to stammer between sobs. "Thank you so much."

"I did it for him as much as you. I don't want to see you die tonight just to have to watch him get tortured and hung tomorrow. There's too much hatred and death in this world and I'm just about tired of it."

"Are you ok?" Benjamin asks as he runs to me.

"Yes, are you?" I ask as I start checking his face and arms for wounds.

"Yes, I landed on a patch of grass. I'm sorry I couldn't protect you. I thought he was going to kill you. I was so scared. Thank goodness Betsy knew what to do. Are you sure you're okay?"

"Yes, I'm sure. Just scared. Thank you for protecting me."

"I didn't, Betsy did."

"You did protect me. You stepped in between us. If you hadn't done that, he would have gotten to me a lot sooner. I wanted to run, but I couldn't make my legs move. You helped save my life, Benjamin. I'm so thankful for you."

A slow drizzle starts to fall. The row is quiet for a moment besides a moan from Ezekiel.

"Is he going to try to hurt you or Betsy when he wakes up?"

"I'm not worried about him. He'll be gone tomorrow. Your brother told me that he and your father are taking him and some other slaves down south."

"That is what I wanted to see you about."

The rain starts to come down harder.

"Come on, come inside," Benjamin says.

We walk into the tiny cabin. The floor is nothing but dirt and there is chinking missing, allowing rain and wind to come in from the outside. There are four cots that look like they have been stuffed with corn husks. I look around and count six people in the cabin.

"Where do you sleep?" I ask.

"I sleep on the floor over in that corner."

"You sleep on the floor, every night?" I ask shocked.

He shrugs. "It stays warm and dry." We walk over and sit down in his corner.

"Why did you want to see me about the shipment of slaves? I'm not going to be sold south, am I?" he asks as he grabs my arm and looks into my eyes. His hands feel so rough. I turn them over to find them torn up and callused from the hard field work. I look up in horror and he quickly pulls his hands away.

"I am so sorry I got you sent down here. I will try to get you back to where you belong, taking care of Shadow and the other horses. I can tell they miss you as much as I do. But no, you are not going to be sold south. I am going to be going south, to Natchez, to live with my grandmother for a while. I wanted to see you one last time before I leave tomorrow."

"How long are you going to be there?"

"I don't know. My mother is hoping that my grandmother can teach me how to be a good, strong, slaveholding woman one day. I don't want to go, but I'm hoping if I go, I can convince my father and mother to bring you back to work with Tom in the stable."

"I'll work in these fields forever if it means I will get to at least be close to you. You are my best friend and I'm going to miss you something awful, Jo."

"I'm going to miss you too, Benjamin."

I stand up with tears streaming down my face and hug him one last time before heading back to the house.

The rain continues to pound against the roof all night as I toss and turn, desperately trying to get some sleep. Between leaving for the unknown tomorrow and having someone try to kill me that evening, rest is not coming easily. I think about Benjamin curled up in the corner of the dirt cabin and how I don't understand why the color of one's skin makes a difference. I must have finally gone to sleep though, because the next thing I know Millie is in my room performing her daily tasks of opening the curtains and bringing clean wash water. The rain is still coming down in sheets and the dreary day is like a smack in the face. I force myself out of bed, wash my face, and get dressed with Millie's unhelpful help. I watch from my window as my trunks are being loaded into the carriage. Tears come to my eyes but I quickly wipe them away. *I can do this,* I tell myself.

I walk downstairs to find my mother eating breakfast by herself. I join her at the table. She tells me that Father and John are out gathering up the slaves that are being transported and that we will have to leave earlier than expected due to the rain making travel more difficult. She then proceeds to talk about what she has planned for her day. My thoughts drift off. *How can my own mother send me away? Has this life she has lived made her heart so cold that she can ship me off like a slave?* One thing I am sure of is that I do not want to turn out like her. I love my mother, but I don't agree with her ways. I want to be more caring and respectful of all people, no matter the color of their skin. Come to think of it, I don't think I have ever heard my mother tell me she loves me. Ann tells me she loves me all the time. Loves me like I was hers she always tells me, and I love her too. Telling my mother that I love her would be awkward.

"Josephine, are you even listening?"

I snap back, "Yes Mother, sorry."

"I said to make sure you give this letter to your grandmother. Tell her I would have loved to have come to visit, but someone must stay here and make sure the slaves get the work done. She should understand. She knows how they lose their way without guidance."

"Yes Mother, I will tell her."

"And you be good for your grandmother. She is a very strong woman and will be able to teach you where I have failed."

"Yes, Mother."

The clanking of chains in the distance ends our conversation.

"Finish up," Mother says. "It'll be time to go soon."

I finish my breakfast and walk out onto the porch. It is so dark and dreary I almost can't stand it. The sky hangs so low it appears to touch the ground. I fight back tears and then I feel an arm around me, Diane's arm. She is going to be traveling with us to visit her mother, my grandmother, who lives in Maysville.

"Are you ready to go on your first adventure?" she asks with enthusiasm as she gives my shoulder a squeeze.

"Yes," I reply trying to imitate her enthusiasm, but failing miserably.

"You will be fine and you will be back home before you know it. I will write to you and let you know everything that is happening in Maysville and when I come back here in the fall to teach your brother, I will keep you updated on everything and everyone," she says with a wink.

"Thank you."

We both climb into the carriage, but before I make it all the way in, I notice that the driver is not as tall as Old Tom. Under those fancy clothes and that top hat is Benjamin! I say a quick prayer thanking God for getting Benjamin out of the fields. I peek out of the carriage and see Tom driving the wagon load of slaves that are too young or old to walk the long way to Maysville. John and Father are on horseback keeping an eye on the other slaves that are chained together and going to be walking the distance. I scan their faces. They all look so hopeless, except one. He is glaring back at me with evil in his eyes, Ezekiel. I shudder and quickly move away from the window thankful that he is being sold and won't be around too much longer. We start to move and I glance back at the house one last time, praying I won't be away too long.

Chapter 13

The journey to Maysville is slow and arduous. The rain made the frequently traveled roads muddy and the other horses and wagons made ruts in the road making it difficult for our carriage and the wagon full of slaves to pass through. Many times, those walking have to push us out of the unforgiving mud. I can hear their chains clanking together as they work. I cannot wait to get out of the carriage and I can imagine those walking want to stop and rest. I can see the sores on some of their ankles and wrists bleeding where their chains rub. Aunt Diane is doing her best keeping me distracted with conversation.

We arrive in Maysville and the number of buildings and people are overwhelming. I have only been to Maysville a couple of times, so I am not used to the crowd. There are carriages everywhere and the closer we move to the center of town, the busier the streets become. Before we reach market street, my father, Lewis the overseer, and the slaves turn down Sutton Street to make their way towards the river and John, Benjamin, Millie, and I continue on towards Limestone Street, where my grandmother moved after my grandfather passed away. She sold the farm and all the slaves. She said she no longer wanted to own another human being. She hired a few maids to cook and clean for her in her new dwelling. We pull up to the house, a large, two-story brick home, too big for one person, but my grandmother wanted to be sure she had plenty of room if any visitors ever came her way. She was quite the socialite in her day, I understand, and still enjoys much company.

Benjamin drops us off at the front door and drives off to the livery stable to feed and water Shadow and allow her to rest before he makes the long trip home. John and I only mean to stop in and see Grandmother for a few minutes, but she insists on providing us with something to eat. She has the young butler run down to fetch my father so he has a good home cooked meal as well. We eat a meal of pork, potatoes, and green beans. It is delicious and my grandmother is so much fun that I do not want to leave, but it is all too soon that my father says it is time to go and get settled into our hotel down by the river. My grandmother pleads with him for us to stay with her, but since our departure is very early and my father still needs to get a few more things straightened out before our trip, he declines the hospitality. I reluctantly hug my aunt and grandmother goodbye and we make our way towards the river to get settled into the hotel.

The town is so busy and noisy with people bustling in and out of shops, the clump of horses' hooves on the dirt streets, and the shouts of men as they holler out orders to their workers. This constant noise makes me miss my quiet home. We make a few stops along the way, my father making sure everything is in order for our departure tomorrow. We finally arrive at our hotel on Front Street. I am exhausted from the long day of traveling. The hotel is quite grand and fairly new. I like the fact that it is right next to the river and I can watch the boats as they pass by. I can't believe that I will be on one tomorrow! My eyes begin to get heavy. I bid my father and brother goodnight and head to my room. Millie helps me into my night clothes. I look around the room and only see one bed.

"Millie, where are you going to sleep?" I ask concerned.

"What's it matter to you?" she responds rather rudely.

"Would you like to share the bed with me, like a sleep over?" I ask excitedly.

"No ma'am, I wouldn't be caught dead in the same bed as you."

I was a little taken back. "Then where are you going to sleep?"

"I sleep on the floor."

"If that's what you want."

I crawl into bed not understanding why she would rather sleep on the floor. No amount of kindness seems to break that girl.

The mattress is harder than I am used too and uncomfortable. *Maybe I should sleep on the floor, too. I wonder what Millie would do if I crawled down next to her on the floor.* The thought makes me giggle to myself. It is with this funny thought that I drift off to sleep only to be awakened not long after.

"Jo, wake up," John whispers.

"What?" The room is chilly and dark so I snuggle further under the covers.

"It will soon be time to board the boat."

I suddenly remember where I am.

"I don't want to go. I belong here, I need to stay."

"Well, I guess you shouldn't have made Mother angry."

"I'm not going! I don't want to go!" I yell.

"Jo, be quiet or you are going to wake everyone else in this hotel. I don't want you to have to stay in Natchez either. I'm going to miss you, but it is what Mother wants. All you have to do is pretend to enjoy the life you have and act like Mother and Grandmother want you to and then you can come back home."

"I don't want to act like Mother. I don't like the way she treats people."

"I don't understand, Jo, she treats others kindly."

"Not slaves."

"That's because slaves are just slaves."

"They are people too, John."

"Then why was Millie sleeping on the floor?"

"I asked her if she wanted to share the bed with me, but she refused."

"You what? Jo, you never cease to amaze me. You'll even let a darkie sleep in your bed. You are something else. One of these days you will grow up and see that they are not like us. Get dressed. Father and I will meet you at the dock. The hotel boy will be in shortly to get your trunks."

Millie helps me get dressed and we head for the dock. The sun has not yet risen and all the townspeople are still sleeping. We meet up with Father and John who are shuffling the slaves down into the hold of the boat. They will be chained down there and only let out at the ports of sale. Millie and I make our way to my room. I open the door and find it is just as fancy as the hotel room. I hop onto the bed, happy to feel that it is more comfortable than the hotel bed. The man who picked up my luggage from the hotel knocked on the door and delivered all of my trunks. Millie began to get things in order. Although I do not like Millie much, I am glad to have her now that I am mostly alone. At least she seems to know what needs to be done. There is a knock on my door.

"Jo?" John's voice comes faintly from the other side of the wood.

"Come in."

"I just wanted to make sure you found your room okay and you are comfortable."

"I am as comfortable as I can be, John, knowing that I am going to a strange place to live." I say as I close my eyes tightly to keep the tears from squeezing out.

"You will be fine, Jo. You're a strong girl and you can handle anything. The way you speak up for what you believe, even if it goes against Mother and Father, that shows you have an inner strength."

"I just hope I don't have to be gone long and Mother lets me come home soon."

"Me too, because I am going to miss you," he pauses, "and all of your questions," he says jokingly with a smile on his face.

I smack his arm, but I can't help but smile back at him. He truly is the best brother a girl could have.

After John leaves, I step out onto the deck. Maysville looks beautiful under the moonlight. I shiver and hug myself. Although it is June the air has been chilly, especially after the rain from yesterday. The steamboats shrill whistle blows and the paddlewheel starts to move as I silently bid my beautiful Kentucky home goodbye and return to my room. I fall into bed and wonder what is to come.

I wake up to the sun shining brightly. I slide out of bed and Millie comes out of nowhere. I didn't even think about where she was going to stay, but it appears she slept on a cot near my bed. She helps me wriggle into my clothes and tells me that Father has stopped by and wants me to come to the dining area when I am ready. I look at myself in the mirror before finally taking a minute to look around the room I will be staying in for the next couple of weeks. The beautiful, wood floor is covered with a soft rug in shades of red and blue. The white walls are adorned with red and blue tapestries to complement the rug. Red, white, and blue is everywhere and the room is beautiful. The steamboat is called the Natchez IV even though it was built in Cincinnati. Many of the previous Natchez ships have exploded, killing the majority of the passengers they carried. I shudder at the thought.

Leaving the comforts of my room, I go in search of the dining room. I find it without much trouble along with my father and John. I sit at the table with them. I made it just in time for lunch. I can't believe that I had slept so late! The meal is delicious and I am happy to spend a little time with Father and John. After eating, Father dismisses himself to spend time with the other men on the ship and John and I go exploring. The ship is massive and everywhere I look there is red, white, and blue, just like my room. We decide to go out on the deck and walk around to get some fresh air. There are many men, women, and children enjoying the sunshine and the fresh air as well. We walk to the stern and watch the paddlewheel as it churns through the water, pushing us closer and closer to our destination. It is mesmerizing watching the wheel turn and I have a feeling I will be spending most of my time watching the paddles push through the water and then roll back around to plunge back into the water again.

The first stop on our trip is Louisville. We stop briefly, pick up several new passengers as well as a few loads of slaves. The slaves are quickly shuffled down to the lower holds of the boat. When we reach Paducah; however, we have several hours to kill. Father and John gather a load of slaves to take to the nearest auction. I decide to go along even though my father protests at first. I tell him I need to learn these things if I am going to be a good slave owner. Father pats me on the head and agrees to let me come along. John looks at me sideways and winks, knowing that I am already playing the game to get back home quicker. We only have to walk a couple of blocks to get to the auction. I have never seen a slave auction before, so I don't quite know what to expect. I watch intently, actually wanting to learn, but not for reasons most people would think. I want to learn everything about slavery so that I will make a good abolitionist one day. The auction begins and it is hard for me to watch. Men, women, and children are brought out onto a stage and examined by various potential buyers. They look them over top to bottom and even put their fingers in their mouths to check to make sure their teeth are healthy. How humiliating that must be for them. I watch as families are split up with crying children being ripped out of their screaming mother's arms. I look away, trying to distract myself to avoid bursting into tears for these people. *How are all these white people so blind? Why can't they see that these people have feelings the same as us?* Then I see them. Faces that look familiar: my father's slaves are up for sale. I watch as many of them are bought and taken away, their faces showing concern and dread at the unknown of what other cruelties they are going to have to endure.

Ezekiel came up for sale, but with the fresh wound on the back of his head he did not sell. I heard my father asking John if he knew how he got that wound, but John said he didn't know. I pray he doesn't ask me because I will have to tell him the truth. I hope Ezekiel sells quickly because he scares me and I want to be as far away from him as possible. I can still see his evil, piercing eyes sometimes when I close my eyes. *Please, please God, please have someone buy Ezekiel at the next port, I pray as we board the boat.* He does not sell at Memphis or Vicksburg. The days get muggier the further south we sail. I continue to pray every day that Ezekiel sells. I do not want him going back to Kentucky where he could hurt Benjamin or Betsy.

By the time we reach Natchez, our destination, Father only has a handful of slaves left. He is happy with the sales so far and is sure that he will be able to unload the rest of his cargo here in Natchez at Forks of the Road market. Ezekiel still hasn't sold and he glares at me as we make our way to the auction block. The auction begins and I watch as the slaves are inspected by the potential buyers. Children run about laughing and playing with each other and ladies hide from the sun underneath their colorful parasols. I wish I had my parasol. I had Millie pack it away, not even thinking that I would be standing out here in the hot sun. My dress is sticking to me and I can feel the sweat trickling down my neck. I thought Kentucky was humid, but it is still morning and it is almost unbearable to be outside here in Natchez. Ezekiel comes up on the block and I can feel his eyes on me. I shiver, even in this heat, as he stares me down. The bidding starts. It always amazes me how people can talk so quickly. I would often pretend to be an auctioneer in my room on the boat. I'm sure it drove Millie crazy, but she never said anything.

"Sold!" cries the auctioneer.

"Thank goodness," I whisper under my breath.

Ezekiel is led off the block to his new master, who quickly shackles him to the other slaves he has just purchased. I hope I never have to see him again.

The auction ends and my father walks away to collect his money. John stands with me chattering about how much money we made. I barely listen, thinking about how hot it is and how I wish I was back home. Tears start to well up in my eyes, but I quickly blink them away when I hear my father's name being shouted.

"Edward!" the man shouts again, "Edward!"

My father turns, walks towards the man, and greets him warmly. He brings him over to John and me and introduces him as our Uncle Charles. He looks a lot like my mother with a slender build and dark brown hair. He leads us to where the buggy is tied and we immediately head to my grandparent's house.

The ride is hot and bumpy. My grandparent's plantation is just on the outskirts of town, so thankfully it doesn't take us long to get there. We turn off the main road onto a lane lined with trees that creates a tunnel for us as we ride along. I have never been more thankful for shade. The trees end and in front of me sits a massive house. I thought my house in Kentucky was big, but this house is massive. It has a porch on the bottom floor that wraps around the whole house as well as a landing on the second floor. The fields seem to go for miles in every direction. From what I can see, it looks like cotton is growing. We are met by my grandparents as the buggy pulls around to the front porch. My grandparents are much older than my grandmother in Maysville. I had learned from John on the trip down here that my grandmother had been married once before to a very wealthy man and he passed away, so my grandmother inherited his money plus married my grandfather, who is a wealthy man in his own right. They had several children together after a few years of marriage, with my mother being the youngest.

John helps me down off the wagon and we enter the massive house. My grandmother has one of the house slaves show me to my room so that I can clean up and change my clothes before lunch. By the time I make it back down, John and my father are already cleaned up and seated at the table. An enormous spread of various foods lay before us. I have never been so happy to see food, because I am famished. I sit down across from my grandmother who is barking orders at the servants. One of the girls walks over to fill my glass with water and spills a tiny drop on the table cloth. I hear her suck in a bit of air and freeze. She looks to be about my age. I smile at her and start to tell her that it is okay, but before I can get my words out, a loud smack makes us all jump. The girl starts to cry. I look to see where the noise came from and I see that it was my grandmother's cane that had hit the table.

"Get over here girl!" my grandmother yells.

The girl reluctantly obeys and walks slowly to my grandmother. Once she reaches where she is seated, she turns with her back to her. My grandmother whacks her twice across her backside with the cane. The tears are now streaming heavily down the girl's face.

"It's okay, Grandmother. It was just a drop and I've already cleaned it up. Please don't punish her anymore," I plead.

My grandmother looks at me with a look of horror on her face. "Charlotte told me I had my work cut out for me, but I did not realize it was going to be this bad. Young lady, these animals need our guidance. If I let her spill that drop of water then the next time it will be two drops and then three and before we know it, she will be spilling the whole pitcher of water onto the table. We must not be lenient and that is something you will learn while you are here. You will also *never* tell me how to treat my slaves again! Do you understand?" she asks with a booming voice.

"Yes ma'am," I manage to stutter, holding back my own tears.

I immediately ask to be excused. I run to my new room and the tears start flowing. *I can't believe I am going to have to stay here when all I want to do is go home.* I sit on the window seat and sob quietly.

I hear Millie quietly say as she unpacks my things, "Now little missy know how we feel when we forced to leave everything we love."

I stand up quickly with fire in my eyes. "I suggest you shut your mouth! You are the reason I am here to begin with. All I wanted to do was teach Benjamin everything that I was learning because he is my friend. I even tried to teach you, but you ruined that. You had to go and tell on us and now we are both stuck here. I am the only one that sees you as a person, while all the rest of my family sees you as a dirty animal, yet you still want to be mean to me. I am just a child and trying to do the best I can to treat you right. Believe me, as soon as I am of age, I will set you free because I want nothing to do with you!"

I slam my face into my pillow and scream with rage. I am upset at my grandmother, at Millie, and at my mother for sending me down here. *My life is falling apart.*

I stay in my room the whole rest of the afternoon, only going downstairs once to say goodbye to my father and John and plead with them to let me go back home. My father kisses me on my head and tells me that this is the best thing for me and that I will be back home soon. John gives me a big hug and says that he loves me and to just obey so I can come home soon.

I watch them drive off from my window with a heavy heart. I slide my hand under my pillow and pull out the cornhusk doll that Benjamin had given me. Holding it tightly, I eventually drift off to sleep.

Chapter 14

I wake up from my troubled sleep and make my way downstairs to join my grandparents for breakfast, filled with dread. The air about the house is very tense and solemn. *Is this how every day of my life here is going to feel?* My grandparents are chatting at the table when I join them and within minutes Uncle Charles comes in and joins the conversation. My uncle has no wife, so he believes it to be his duty to take care of the family plantation. He will take over completely after my grandparents pass on.

I learn that my plans for today are to take a tour through the house as well as a trip into Natchez to learn my way around the area. Since I am close enough, grandmother has informed me that I am going to be attending school in town. This news turns my stomach into knots. I have never been to a real school before. I have always been with my brother and taught at home. I don't want to go to school, but I stay quiet, because I don't think arguing will do me any good.

Everyone finishes eating and the men head out to oversee that the work is getting done properly and my grandmother begins to show me around the house. The house is the biggest one I've ever seen. There are no less than 15 rooms downstairs and the foyer has two grand staircases on each side that curve around to meet each other on the second floor. There are just as many rooms upstairs and they are all adorned with the most beautiful and ornate pieces of furniture and tapestries. We step out onto the veranda on the second floor and my grandmother points out how far each way their property extends. There is so much land that I can barely see where it ends! In the distance I can see the city of Natchez and I can hear the whistle of the steamships as they leave port. I struggle to hold back tears as I think of my father and brother being on one of those ships headed back home without me.

We eat a light lunch and then began our trip into town. My grandmother and I discuss all sorts of things and she tells me a great deal about her life and what it is like living in Natchez. I find myself laughing and smiling a lot as we walk through the city streets. *How can this be the same woman from yesterday?* We drive past the schoolhouse where I will be spending my winter days, the church that we will be attending every Sunday, and the mansions of some of the most notable people that reside here. We walk through just about every store so that by the time we loop back around to the buggy my legs can barely move. We load the buggy up with our purchases and squeeze in beside them, ready for our trip back home. What an enjoyable day! I can't wait to get back and write about it in my journal. As soon as the driver pulls up to the front door, I quickly hug my grandmother and rush upstairs to my room for the night.

I am awakened by a crack of thunder. I roll over to see a fierce rain beating hard against the panes of glass. For a minute I think they may shatter. Lightning flashes, thunder rolls, and I am afraid the wind may blow the whole house down. I race downstairs in fright.

"Grandmother, are we going to be okay?" I ask trembling.

She smiles and gives me a hug. "Yes, child, we are just fine. This house has weathered many a storm like this one. Your uncle can read the skies well and there are no tornadoes in sight."

I let out a breath of relief and my nerves calm a little until another bolt of lightning hits followed by its crack of thunder. I jump up with a shriek and everyone starts to laugh.

"Josephine," my grandmother says in a very serious tone. "Young ladies must be strong no matter what. Show no fear, even when you may be scared to death. You will battle many storms throughout your life, but you must always meet them head on with fierce determination. There are so many weak people in this world, especially women, that falter under the least bit of adversity. You will not be one of them. Do you understand?"

I look at my grandmother in amazement. I can see her strength as she sits there straight and tall. Even though she is old, she maintains a strength and a confidence that I can feel. My mother carries that same air about her. I know now that I want that strength as well.

"Yes, Grandmother. I do understand."

"Good. And since there is nothing we can do right now but wait out the storm, let's go over what else it is you need to learn while you are here. The main thing that I need to teach you is how to control the negroes. As you can see, they are not like us," she says as she motions around the room at the negroes that are bustling about performing their various tasks. "They are dumb and without our guidance they would be lost."

"But Grandmother, they aren't dumb. They can learn just like us."

"I heard you taught a boy to read and write. What were you thinking, Josephine?"

"He's my friend and I wanted to see if what everyone was telling me was true. I wanted to see if negroes were really dumb or if they could be taught to read and write."

"They can be taught, Josephine. They can be taught to do what we want them to know and do, but that doesn't mean they are smart."

"It doesn't?" I ask with curiosity.

"No. They can learn with our guidance, but if you put negroes out to live by themselves, they would never make it on their own without us showing and telling them what to do. That is why God has given us the strength to not only take care of ourselves, but the negroes as well. It is our duty as good Christian men and women. That is why it is important for you to gain an inner strength so that you can take care of yourself, your husband, and the negroes. Do you understand?"

"Sort of."

"Don't you take care of Millie?"

"Well, she takes care of me mostly, it seems. She helps me get dressed and cleans up after me."

"She has been taking care of you because you were young. Your mother has been giving Millie the guidance that she needs. You are getting older Josephine and it is your responsibility to take care of her now, especially since you are away from home.

"I don't know if I can treat them the way you and mother do."

"How do you think we treat them?"

"Well," I start rather sheepishly, "it seems like you are mean to them."

110

Grandmother lets out a laugh. "It is for their own good. If we let them get away with things, they will walk all over us, just like any dumb animal would. Take a horse. If you don't discipline and train it, it will be unruly and could potentially hurt you. It is the same situation with the negroes."

I think for a minute. Millie pulls my hair hard while fixing it because I am not training her not to. I am not doing my duty towards her.

"Are you understanding this, Josephine."

I smile at her. "Yes, this is starting to make sense to me."

I pause for a minute, though, thinking about all the tears and anguish that I saw from the negroes as they were bought, sold, and torn apart from their families.

"I may be able to do my duty as a southern woman to take care of the slaves, but I don't think I could ever buy or sell a slave."

"You may be too young to have experienced this, but haven't you ever wished a slave was out of your hair because they were lazy or mean, and when they were gone, you were relieved and happy?"

Immediately Ezekiel popped into my mind. "Yes, actually I have."

She smiles, "Well, young lady, you are on your way to being a fine southern woman."

I smile back and think about this for a moment. *Maybe I am not so different from my family after all.* The lightning cracks, and this time, I don't even flinch.

Chapter 15

The days and months continue to pass by, and although a part of me still misses my Kentucky home, I am in a comfortable routine at Natchez. I watch my grandmother every day, admiring how she runs the household and I hope I can be half as good as her one day. She never appears to crack under any type of pressure.

Grandmother and I are taking tea in the parlor one afternoon when my grandfather comes in with the mail from town. Grandmother begins to shuffle through as I wait patiently to see if there is a letter for me from home. She pauses on one letter.

"What does it say?" I ask curiously.

"We are cordially invited to the Gerard Plantation for their annual 4th of July Picnic. This will be good for you, Josephine. It will allow you to mingle with some of the children whom you will be attending school."

My heart sinks. I hated going to parties back home and now I won't even have Mary to talk to.

"Must I go, Grandmother? I really don't like going to parties."

"Yes, young lady, you must. You will be attending numerous parties during your stay here, because we get invited to many and we must attend due to our status within society."

"I understand," I mumbled.

The 4th of July comes all too quickly for me. I put my best party dress on with Millie's help and try to prepare myself for my first picnic without Mary. I am so nervous I can barely eat breakfast. In due time, my grandparents and I climb into the buggy and we head towards the Gerard Plantation. It's a beautiful day and I try to calm my nerves by watching the birds fly across the cloudless sky.

We arrive at the plantation and although grandmother allows me to go off on my own and mingle, I decide to stay close to her and people watch. I glance around and see all sorts of men and women in their finest attire talking and laughing with one another. Groups of children are clumped under the shade trees playing various games. I notice one group of children staring at me and snickering. I quickly look away from them and I see a girl walking towards me. She has brown hair and hazel eyes and appears to be a little taller than me. My heart starts to beat faster as she nears. Surely she is not coming over to me.

"Hello. I'm Elizabeth," she greets warmly.

"Hello. I'm Josephine," I respond shyly.

"I already know your name. News around here travels quickly."

I glance over and see the other children still snickering at me.

"Oh, don't worry about them," Elizabeth says as she sees who I am looking at. "They make fun of everyone who hasn't lived here their whole life. They make fun of me all the time because my family and I moved here from France a few years ago. You would think they would get tired of it, but they don't," she says with a shrug. "I'm glad you came. Usually I am all alone. The other kids don't like to play with me because I am not one of them as they say and because I am an aspiring artist and they don't understand why I enjoy drawing so much."

"You can draw?" I ask amazed.

"Yes, and very well too. Here, let me show you," she says as she picks up a stick and begins to draw in the dirt.

I join in picking up my own stick.

"You are good! Your people actually look like people. Mine just look like blobs," I say in amazement.

"Elizabeth! Young ladies do not play in the dirt. How many times must I tell you?"

Elizabeth and I both jump up, dusting our dresses off quickly.

"Sorry, Mother. I was just showing Josephine how well I can draw."

"It is nice to meet you, Josephine, but young ladies must not play in the dirt."

"Yes ma'am," I agree.

We both look at each other as her mother walks away and giggle.

"Where do you live?" I ask curious.

"In town above my family's store which sells many different commodities as well as my paintings."

"I can't wait to see all of your paintings one day."

"You'll have to come to the store sometime and I will show you."

The time at the party flies by and it isn't long before the fireworks are lighting up the night sky.

"This is the best 4th of July I've ever had," Elizabeth says beaming as she squeezes my hand.

I squeeze back and smile, "Me too."

The summer is winding down and school will soon be

starting. I dread the thought of going to school. I have never been in a classroom with anyone other than my brother. I continue to plead with my grandmother not to make me go, but she won't budge. I have worried myself half sick. I worry the other kids will make fun of me, because they never made any attempt to come over and talk to me at the parties. I worry that the teacher will be mean. I really enjoyed being taught by my Aunt Diane last year and I wished she was teaching me again this year. The thought of home, my brother, and aunt just about brings me to tears. Grandmother says crying is for babies though, so I quickly get up and head out to the stable to distract myself from thoughts of home. The horses do the trick. It doesn't take long before I am laughing at them as they compete for my attention. I stay until the sun sets and then head back to my room hoping tomorrow won't come.

I roll over and realize as I open my eyes that today is my first day of school. I suddenly can't move. I am paralyzed in fear.

"Come on Miss Josephine. Your grandmother say it time for you to get up now and get ready for school. I's supposed to fix your hair extra nice today for your first day," Millie says as she enters my room.

I groan and slowly roll out of bed. Millie helps me get dressed and then starts to fix my hair. She starts pulling as hard as usual, but today I am not in a very good mood and I am not about to put up with it.

"Millie, please don't pull so hard."

"I's just trying to fix your hair like your grandmother wants."
She pulls even harder.

"Millie, I'm not going to tell you again. Please stop pulling so hard."

I feel a good hard tug on my hair. I can't stop myself. Fuming,

I turn around and without thinking slap Millie across her face.

"I said stop pulling!"

Millie looks at me with wide eyes and her hand flies up to her cheek, rubbing where I just slapped.

I turn back around, "Now, fix my hair without pulling it!"

I continue to sit in the chair as Millie finishes fixing my hair. I don't know if she is pulling it or not. I can't feel anything. I feel numb. I just hit someone. This is what I have watched my grandmother do the last several months and my mother in the years prior. I came to believe this was an inner strength, but I don't feel good about doing it. I don't feel empowered or that I have helped Millie in any way. I am so confused and now on top of everything, I have to go to my first day of school.

The buggy bounces along the dirt road as we make our way into town. It's just me and Alexander, the driver. I watch the butterflies flit about and I wish to be one of them. I would much rather be flying from one beautiful, sweet smelling flower to another all day than going to school. Before I know it, the fields that line the road turn into houses and the road becomes congested with other buggies and wagons with people going about their daily tasks. Alexander pulls up to the school house.

"All right little Missy, this be yo' stop."

"Thank you, Alexander," I say meekly as I look out at the schoolhouse grounds, where many of the children are either huddled in groups playing marbles or tearing through the grass in a game of chase.

I climb out of the buggy, straighten my dress, and head towards the schoolhouse door.

"There she is. She's the new girl that likes negroes," I hear someone whisper.

I keep walking, picking up my pace and ignoring the whispers and stares. Just as I am ascending the steps, the teacher steps out and begins ringing the bell to start the day.

"You must be Josephine," she says smilingly sweetly.

"Yes ma'am," I manage to say.

"I'm Mrs. Boudreaux. Please go on in and find a seat."

I walk in and thankfully find Elizabeth in a seat drawing a picture of Mrs. Boudreaux. I slide in next to her.

"Good morning Jo," she greets cheerily.

"Good morning. You're drawing is very good. It looks just like our teacher."

"Thank you."

I want to talk more, but Mrs. Boudreaux quiets the room down and we begin our studies.

After a couple hours of reading and arithmetic, it is time for recess. Elizabeth and I walk outside to enjoy the fresh air, even though it is hot and muggy.

"What are you doing playing with that negro lover, Elizabeth?" a freckle faced boy asks.

"Leave us alone," she responds.

"Why do you like negroes, Josephine, is it because they are as dirty and smelly as you?"

Another boy chimes in, "Frederick, leave the girl alone."

"But she's a negro lover."

"I am not."

"How do you know she likes negroes?" One of the girls asks.

"My mother told me. She taught one of them how to read and write. Her mother sent her down here so that her grandmother can rid her of the devil and turn her into a Christian woman. If you ask me, I think she oughta be hung just like those dirty darkies that she loves so much."

"Well it's not up to you, Frederick, so go away and leave her alone," Elizabeth screams.

Just then, the bell rings. *Thank goodness,* I silently sigh in relief.

As I walk into the schoolhouse with Elizabeth, Frederick whispers in my ear, "You say you aren't a negro lover, you'll have to prove it."

I don't know how I am supposed to prove it and I can barely focus on my studies because of it. I just pray that Alexander will be waiting for me with the buggy at the end of the day.

The afternoon flies by, unfortunately, and as soon as the teacher dismisses us, I bid Elizabeth farewell and hurry towards the door. I no sooner make it out the door and down the steps when I fall hard to the ground, bumping my forehead. I hear some of the other children snicker. I roll over slowly to see what I had tripped over. It doesn't take me long to figure it out. Frederick is there looking down upon me and laughing. I jump up.

"Why did you trip me?"

"Me, I would never do such a thing, but since I have your and everybody's attention, I want you to prove to me that you are not a negro lover."

I dust my dress off, stand up straight and tall, and declare, "I am not a negro lover. I don't know how to prove it to you, but just take my word on the matter."

"That's not what I heard about you. You taught one to read and write. You're nothing but a traitor. Once they learn to read and write, they think they can do anything. Start asking why they are being held as slaves, then they get the idea to run away or slit our throats at night."

"Benjamin would never do anything like that," I say shocked.

"His name is Benjamin, eh? So, what my mother told me is the truth! Ladies and gentlemen, this girl is a negro lover! From now on, anyone that talks to her will be deemed dirty white trash."

"No, please," I cry. "I am not a negro lover! I am no different than all of you."

I look at the faces around me and many of them just shake their heads.

"Prove it," Frederick says with a smirk on his face.

"How?"

"Samuel, come here!"

I turn to look and I see a black boy hop off a buggy and run towards us.

"Yes, Massa?"

"Josephine, this is Samuel, one of my family's slaves," He says as he picks up a stick and hands it to me. "If you are like all the rest of us, you shouldn't have any trouble with this. Hit him."

"What?" I ask shocked.

"Take this stick and hit him."

The boy looks at me with eyes wide.

"He is not my property," I say hoping to diffuse the situation.

"I give you my permission, now hit him."

"But he did nothing wrong."

"He is a dirty slave. He doesn't have to do anything wrong. Prove that you are one of us and hit him!" he demands more forcefully.

I look around at everyone as they start to jeer and chant along with Frederick.

"Josephine loves darkies! Josephine loves darkies!"

"Stop it, please." A mixture of anger and sadness begins to well up inside me. *I just want to fit in. Why can't I just hit him? I hit Millie this morning. Yes, I think, but she pulled my hair. She deserved it. But, did she really deserve it? Isn't this who I am trying to be, someone like my grandmother, a good southerner. Just a couple of whacks. I'm sure it won't even hurt the boy.* I can still hear the chants from the other children and can see Frederick just to the left of me making faces. I grip the stick tight, pull my arm back, and bring it down hard. WHACK! WHACK! WHACK! Each hit is harder and harder and as the boy yells out, I feel stronger and stronger. Before I am finished, someone grabs me from behind.

"Miss Josephine, Miss Josephine. What are you doing?"

I drop the stick and look down at Frederick whose eye is already starting to turn black from getting hit by the stick.

"He was calling me names and he tripped me," I say.

"I see little missy. You do have a right smart bump on your head. Come on Missy, let's get you to the buggy and get you home."

I walk with Alexander to the buggy, not exactly sure what to make of what just happened, but feeling stronger than I ever have.

Alexander helps me up into the wagon and the reality of what I'd done hits me. "I just hit Frederick."

"Yes, little missy, I's saw ya. You were a wailing on him pretty good."

"When my grandmother catches wind of this, she is going to be angry with me. And besides that, none of the other children at school are going to want to speak to me ever again. They ignore me already as it is. What am I going to do?"

"Well now, I's don't rightly know, but you may want to ask Delilah. She always good at answering our questions."

"Who's Delilah?"

"You ain't met Delilah? She seem to know a lot about you. Say you a troubled girl, being pushed and pulled in two different directions, and if you don't get it together, it gonna tear you apart, she say."

"She does seem to know me well. Where can I find her?"

"She live in da same house as you. Only negro your grandmother let stay in da big house. She growed up wit your grandmother and been taking care of her all her life, but she also help keep an eye on the children down on slave row as well as all the other tasks around da house. She prolly know just as much about what goes on at the plantation as your grandparents. I'm surprised you ain't talked to her."

I am surprised too, but I have been so focused on learning from my grandmother that I have pretty well ignored everyone else. Come to think of it, this is the first time that I have spoken with Alexander and he has driven us to many a party and picnic.

Alexander pulls the buggy up to the front door and helps me climb down. I am hoping to sneak past my grandmother. I do not want her to ask me how my day went, because I will have to tell her the truth, and I am not ready for that yet.

I walk through the front door quietly and start to climb the stairs.

"Young lady!"

I stop dead in my tracks, heart pounding.

"Yes ma'am," I say as I descend the stairs and head into the dining parlor where my grandmother is seated.

"Sit down," she commands as she motions with her cane towards the nearest chair.

Now I know how the slaves feel when my grandmother addresses them. I am scared to death.

"I heard something very disturbing just a few minutes ago about your day at school. Would you like to tell me your side of the story?"

News does travel fast around here, I think.

I let everything spill out quickly about how Frederick was being mean and he tripped me and got everyone in school to call me names and I just couldn't take it anymore, so I hit him with a stick.

There is a long pause as she digests my story. I wait anxiously, wondering what she will do to me. Finally, she looks at me and smiles.

"Frederick has always been a pompous boy and I am glad you did not let him walk all over you. However, I do not condone hitting. My other concern is the fact that you did not provide the same fate to the little darkie boy."

"But he didn't do anything to me, Grandmother."

"It does not matter. You should have proved to the others that you are not what they call you. I do not want you to taint our good name."

"Yes, Grandmother, I'm sorry."

"Come here, child, let me look at that bump on your head."

She kisses it and says that should take care of it. I smile back at her and dismiss myself and head to my room.

I sit on the window seat looking out at the fields and watch as the slaves harvest the cotton. Whoever Delilah is, she is right, I am being torn apart. On the one hand I have my family, whom I never want to disappoint. I never really cared until I came down here and met my grandmother. She carries an inner fire that I want to possess. On the other hand, is the fact that I don't agree with owning another person; however, I do own Millie. I am a slave owner. But it wasn't my choice, my father bought Millie for me. I slam my face into the pillow confused. I need to find Delilah. She seems to know a lot about me, so maybe she can help me figure myself out.

I venture around the house looking for Delilah, but can't seem to find her, so I make my way outside. Even though the sun is about to set and it is nearing October, it is still muggy. I walk around to the kitchen behind the house. There are several house slaves eating and chatting amongst themselves. Everyone seems so lively and happy, much different from how they act amongst white people. I knock at the entrance and the room instantly falls silent when they catch sight of me.

"What is she doing here?" someone whispers.

An older woman with caramel colored skin and beautiful brown eyes rises from her chair, "Come in child. What can I help you with?"

I hesitantly step into the room. I realize that all of these people look familiar. I have seen them every day since I arrived, but I don't know a single one of their names.

"I'm looking for Delilah," I stammer.

The woman smiles, "Well child, you have found her. I have been waiting for you. Come, let's take a walk."

She puts her arm around me as we make our way down the garden path. The flowers that are still in bloom glow in the setting sun and let off a sweet fragrance. I don't really know what to say, so we walk in silence for a minute.

"Are we going to walk across this whole plantation or are you going to start talking?" Delilah asks with a little chuckle.

I giggle nervously. There is something so familiar about her, yet I can't quite put my finger on it. It is this familiarity that allows me to open up to her. I tell her everything. I tell her about teaching Benjamin to read and write and about hitting

123

Millie this morning. I also tell her about Frederick and how I hit him with a stick after school. I tell her my whole family wants me to carry on our name as a good, strong, slaveholding woman and that I don't know what to do or how to act and that I feel I am being torn apart.

"I feel like my whole world is just one big mess," I finish, surprised at how long I have talked.

Delilah stops walking and engulfs me in a big hug. She lets me go and as we start walking again, she says, "You are too young to have to be dealing with such difficulty, but God would not have given you this burden if He did not think you could handle it. Let me ask you. How did you feel when you were teaching Benjamin to read and write?"

"I was happy. Benjamin is my best friend. I miss him so much. We used to talk about everything and play and explore the creek whenever we had a chance." I smile just thinking about him.

"And when you hit Millie, how did you feel?"

"For a split second, I felt good, but then I felt sad, like I did something wrong."

"Why did you feel good for that split second?"

"Well, I felt good because I finally acted as the rest of my family would have and it made me feel like I belonged. Millie is always being mean to me and it felt good to finally get back at her, but then I looked at her and I saw the shock and pain in her eyes, and that made me sad."

"How did you feel when you hit Frederick?"

I look up at her and smile, "That felt good and still does. He is mean. Not only to me, but other people as well. He deserved what I gave him."

She chuckles, "Josephine, I can't tell you how to act or what to do or not do, but I can tell you one thing and that is to follow your heart. Anyone can tell you to act a certain way, but you will not be truly happy unless you are following what is in your own heart."

"But how can I follow what's in my heart when my family is constantly against how I feel?"

"That is a difficult situation that will get easier once you are older and can go your own way. Right now, all you can do is pray to the good Lord for guidance. Like I said, He will not give you any more than you can handle."

I think for a moment. "I don't know if that is true."

"What do you mean, child?"

"Look what He has done to you. He has made you my grandmother's slave. You have no freedom. Haven't you ever wanted to be free?"

"Of course, child. Everyone wants to be free and be able to go and do as they please. I have had my words with the good Lord, believe me. Especially when he allowed my baby girl to be taken away from me."

"I'm sorry to hear about your baby. What did she die from?"

"She didn't die. My baby was sold about ten years ago now when she was with child and I haven't seen her since. I was never so upset with your grandmother and the Lord."

"Why were you upset with my grandmother?"

"Because she was the one that sold my daughter. She said that my daughter was useless here since she was with child, but she could be sold as a wet nurse for a nice price. I begged with her to keep her and to not separate us, but she didn't listen. I prayed to the Lord that your grandmother would change her mind, but she didn't. I was mad at the both of them, but I have prayed and prayed that I would be able to see my daughter again and then you came to the plantation and I knew that my prayers had, in the Lord's way, been answered."

I look at Delilah not understanding. "How does my staying here answer your prayers?"

"You see, child, my daughter's name is Ann. She was sold to be a wet nurse, your wet nurse."

I don't know what to say. I have never thought about Ann having any family besides Benjamin.

"I'm sorry I was born and the reason your daughter was taken from you."

"Oh no! Don't you ever say that. You have been a blessing. If it wasn't for you, she would have been sold off to who knows where. At least I knew where she went and your father would tell me how she was doing on his trips down here."

"I still don't understand how my being here brings you any closer to your daughter or grandson."

"I'm not exactly sure how yet either, but I know the Lord has a plan and you being here feels like I am closer to getting back to her than ever before."

"I'm not sure what to do, but I'll do whatever I can to help."

"Pray, child, that is all we can do for each other is pray. Open our hearts to the good Lord and he will guide us and take us where we are supposed to go."

We walk in silence back to the house, but before we get too close, I stop and give Delilah a hug and thank her for talking to me. I walk in first and head to my room. I go straight to my trunk and retrieve my corn husk doll. I have not had it out in months and I am disappointed in myself for trying to be someone I am not. I lie down in bed, hold it tightly, thinking of all the good times that Benjamin and I have had and hoping we will be back together again soon. I pray to the Lord that

I can find a way to bring Ann and Delilah back together. I also pray that I will never falter again and always stay true to myself and my beliefs, no matter what happens.

Chapter 16

I awake before sunrise dreading the fact that I have to go back to school. I work through the motions of my morning routine with a sick feeling in my stomach. When Alexander pulls up with the buggy, my legs turn to lead. Alexander must have seen the dread on my face, because he tells me not to worry and that he will hang around after he drops me off until Ms. Boudreaux rings the bell to make sure Frederick doesn't bother me. I thank him and to take my mind off school, I make conversation with Alexander. He tells me that he had been born and raised on my grandparent's plantation and took over as the driver when Henry, the previous driver, passed away. He enjoys taking care of the horses and being able to go to different places and meet new people. Our conversation ends too early as the schoolhouse comes into view.

"I's be right here if ya need me," Alexander assures me as I slowly exit the buggy.

"Thank you," I say as I start walking hesitantly towards the schoolhouse.

I walk by the kids playing outside and some of them stop to stare at me. I step into the schoolhouse where Elizabeth waves me over to sit next to her.

"I was afraid you wouldn't want me to sit with you anymore,"

I say.

"Why?" she asks looking confused.

"Because of what I did to Frederick yesterday."

"He deserved it, he's mean. I am glad you hit him. You probably won't have to worry about any of the other kids picking on you anymore either. They are scared of you now," she informs me with a smile.

"Well, at least I still have you as a friend," I reply as I return her smile.

Elizabeth is right. All of the little kids are afraid of me and most of the older kids, like Frederick just ignore me, which is fine by me. I just hope it lasts until I go back home to Kentucky, which I hope is soon. I love my grandparents very much, but I long to talk to Benjamin, my family, and ride Shadow through the woods again. The only thing that is keeping me from asking my grandmother if I can return home is the fact that I still need to find a way to bring Delilah and Ann back together again. I am thinking about this dilemma during arithmetic when an idea pops into my mind. *This has to work,* I think excitedly.

I run up to my room as soon as I arrive back at my grandparent's house, grab a piece of parchment paper, and begin to write.

Dear Mother, Father, and John,

I hope this letter finds you well. Christmas is coming, and since I have never been away from my family on that blessed day, I was hoping that you all could make the special trip down here to spend it with all of us in Natchez. I know that Mother has not been down here in years and Grandmother would love to see her again. She talks about you often.

I love you all and please give Shadow a big hug and an apple for me. Tell her I miss her so much.

Love,

Josephine

If Mother came down here, I know she would bring Ann. She would be lost without her and that would finally bring Delilah and Ann back together again. I smile at my plan. This would have to work.

Every day after school I ask if a letter has arrived for me and every day, I get the same answer: no. Christmas is next week. If this doesn't work, I am at a loss. I pray and pray that the letter will come soon.

It is midway through the week before Christmas and still no letter. I walk into the house expecting the same, when my grandfather hands me not only a letter, but a package as well.

I quickly run to my room to open the letter and box.

Dear Josephine,

We would love nothing more than to come see you, but there has been one snow storm after another here and the roads are impassable for a traveling family. We sent Benjamin out with this letter and box of gifts for you in the hopes that you will receive it before Christmas.

Love,

All of us

My heart sinks. I open the box to find a doll, some clothes, and a transparent tart that Frannie had made. She makes the best transparent tarts, but I just can't bring myself to eat it yet. Underneath everything, at the bottom of the box, is a note. I pull it out and begin reading:

Dear Jo,

Yur mother sent me to the post office with dis box of gifts, so I was able to sneek in dis note. I miss you a lot. Life here just ain't the same without you. I ben taking good care of Shadow. I kin tell she misses you too. I wuld like to write more, but I need to get dis to the post office before Shadow and me both freeze. I hope you are gittin along good down there and making lots of new frinds.

Merry Christmas Jo!

Your best frind,

Benjamin

Tears start to fall. Not only because I miss home, but because my plan failed. *Why did God send the snow storms when I have been praying so hard for this plan to work?* I don't understand. I take my cornhusk doll out from its hiding place in my trunk, curl up on my bed, and try to think of a new plan until I fall asleep.

Christmas has come and gone as well as January and February. Nothing seems to change. I go to school and continue to pray for a way to help Delilah. I write often to my Aunt Diane. It is one of the ways I am able to write to Benjamin. My aunt lets him write to me on her parchment paper so he won't get caught. I am writing a new letter to them when I hear a knock on my door.

"Josephine?"

"Yes, Grandmother? Come in."

"I've been watching you," she says as she works her way over to the chair in my room.

My heart starts to pound. Did she see me talking too friendly to Delilah or Alexander? I try to fake being stern with all the negroes when she is around. I made sure that all the house slaves knew that I had to act in this way or I would never get to go back home. They understood and hopefully forgave me when I had to speak harshly to them. The only one who wouldn't forgive me, I'm sure, is Millie. She will probably hate me until the day that I die.

131

"I believe you have made a big improvement in the time that you have been here. I feel that if you would like to go home, you may, and that your mother will be proud of the way you have turned out. I feel that any southern gentleman will be glad to call you his wife when the time comes," she smiles proudly.

"Thank you, Grandmother."

"I'll write a letter to your mother and make the necessary arrangements tomorrow."

I get to go home. I start to get up and holler for Millie to help me pack my belongings when I think about Delilah. I still haven't figured out what to do about her and Ann. It will have to wait though. Right now, all I want to do is go home. I open my trunk and pull out the cornhusk doll, do a little dance, kiss it, and put it right back in its hiding spot. My joy feels endless. Tomorrow can't come soon enough.

Chapter 17

"Josephine! Josephine!" Delilah's voice sounds anxious.

I shoot up out of bed. It's too early for school. I don't know what is going on. I run to my bedroom door and Delilah is there.

"There is something wrong with your grandmother."

I race downstairs to the dining room where my grandmother is lying on the floor. My grandfather is already there, looking at me worriedly.

I grab my grandmother's hand and squeeze, but she doesn't squeeze back. I look at her face and notice that one side looks like it has melted. I ask her if she is okay and she tries to answer me, but she can't seem to form her words.

Alexander fetches the doctor and he examines my grandmother. From what he gathered from his exam and what my grandfather said happened, he says he figures it is something called apoplexy and that she may recover somewhat from the incident. He says the best thing for her now is plenty of rest.

Grandfather and I get my grandmother to her bed and tuck her in. I go back to my room to try and get some rest. I know it won't be much, because the sun is already starting to peak over the horizon. I must have fallen asleep, though, because I am awakened by my Aunt Theresa and Uncle Charles as they make their way up the stairs to see my grandmother. I get dressed on my own, not having the slightest idea where Millie is. It seems like she is around less and less these days and I have heard word that she has found a beau down on slave row. I walk into my grandparent's room to find my grandmother sitting up in bed. She seems to be speaking a little better and the right side of her face doesn't appear to be melting as bad as it did last night. Her face is only droopy around her right eye now.

"Good morning, Josephine," my uncle greets.

"Good morning, Uncle Charles and Aunt Theresa. How are you feeling, Grandmother?"

"I'm doing better, child, thank you. Josephine, dear, I know I told you that you could go home, but I was wondering if you could stay awhile longer to help me out. It appears that my right leg is being difficult and doesn't want to move with me. A loving face to help me out every day would do me good."

My heart sinks. I feel sad for my grandmother. I want to help her out, but I really want to go back home more.

"Why can't Aunt Theresa help you?" I ask.

"I would love to, but I have my own children and house to manage. I will still try to come over every day, but I can't make any promises," Aunt Theresa replies.

"I understand. Yes, Grandmother, I will stay as long as you need me." Deep down, I am hoping I won't be needed for very long.

The days turn into months and they consist of school and helping my grandmother around the house. The movement in her leg has come back a little bit and she is able to get around with the help of her cane, but not as good as she used to. When she wants to go to town, I assist her and I help her move around on the uneven surfaces. I also help steady her when we go to various parties and picnics. She does not like to be seen as weak, so she tries to disguise her lameness as much as possible. This is where I come in, being her stable structure and voice when needed. I don't mind it, I rather like helping her, but I still miss home. Everything is starting to become quite monotonous.

I wake up to sunshine and birds singing and realize it's my birthday. *I'm twelve years old today. Two years ago, I was waking up in Kentucky and realizing just how terrible the world really is. I pray this birthday will be much better.*

"Good morning, Millie." I greet her as she walks into my room looking as gloomy as ever.

"If you think so. Same as any other day for me."

She helps me get dressed and I go to see if my grandmother needs anything. She has already made her way downstairs with Delilah's help.

"Good morning, everyone," I exclaim as I enter the dining room.

"Good morning, Josephine. Happy birthday," my grandparents reply together.

"Josephine, we will have a hearty breakfast of eggs, grits, and sausage and then we will head into town and you can buy whatever your heart desires," Grandfather says.

"Anything," I asked shocked.

"Yes, anything you want," he replies.

"Thank you so much," I reply graciously.

Everything is so enticing I can hardly choose, but I finally decide on a new white parasol to keep the hot sun from scorching my face as well as a couple of new dresses. We pick up Elizabeth from her house and return home for a nice luncheon. Elizabeth and I enjoy the rest of the day together chatting and exploring the plantation. It is a relaxing and fun day that ends all too quickly. Alexander and I take Elizabeth back to her house in the evening and then I settle into my room to write letters home to tell them all about my birthday. I am just finishing up my last letter to my Aunt Diane when I hear a noise outside. I have my window open trying to catch the slightest breeze because it is so hot and muggy, even after the sun has set. I poke my head out of the window and listen intently. *It sounds like someone crying.* I lean further out the window but can't see anything or anyone. *It is probably just a raccoon,* I think as I shimmy my upper half back inside. I head back to my writing desk, but before I make it, I hear it again. It definitely isn't a raccoon. My curiosity gets the better of me and I can't stand not knowing. I have to find out who or what it is. I creep down the stairs and outside into the night.

The lack of moonlight makes it very difficult to see. I try to follow the sound, stopping and holding my breath every so often. It sounds like it is coming from the rose of Sharon bushes near the shed. I pick up the nearest stick I can find just in case it really is an animal and, walking around, find a gap to peak in. Just as I grab a branch to pull it back, an owl screeches. I jump back with a gasp and immediately the noise stops. With trembling hands, I grab the branch again, take a couple of deep breaths and pull it back. Nothing moves or makes a sound, so I peek my head in to get a better look. What I see startles me more than the owl. There are two sets of eyes peering back at me belonging to two small children.

"What are you doing in here?" I whisper.

One starts to sniffle again and the other just looks back at me.

"It's okay, please don't cry. Come on out, it's okay," I coax.

Finally, one of the children comes out and the other follows. They can't be any older than five or six and they are so skinny that their raggedy clothes just hang off of them.

"Why are you hiding in the bushes?" I ask.

There is a long pause, but finally one of the little boys speaks up saying, "We ran away from our mean massa, but he sic the dogs after us, so momma told us to go one way and she went da other. We don't know where to go and we scared."

My eyes widen. *These are runaway slaves!* I look around quickly.

"I don't know what to do," I whisper.

"Please don't hurt us and don't take us back to our massa. He'll hang us like he hung our daddy."

"I won't do either." *What was I going to do, though? I can't harbor fugitive slaves!*

"Ami," the crying child says.

"What?"

"Ami," he repeats.

"Dat be the password our momma tell us to remember to tell the people at da house, so they take us to safcty," the other one explains.

Ami. Ami. Why does that sound so familiar? And then it clicks - it's the French word for friend. Elizabeth has been teaching me French words and phrases and *ami* is always one she told me I had to remember, because it is important to many different people. I didn't understand what she meant until now.

"Are you going to take us back to our massa?"

"No, I am going to take you to safety." *At least I hope I am.* "Stay here, I'll be right back."

I run to the barn and grab Buckeye, my favorite horse, and

quietly head back to the bushes. I help each child mount and then nestle in between them, telling them both to be quiet and to hang on. I nudge Buckeye lightly to get her to start walking and once we are far enough away from the house, I give her a quick kick with my heels and we careen down the road. I pray we will not run into anyone and I keep my ears open for the sound of dogs. It feels like an eternity, but we finally make it to town. I ride around to the back of Elizabeth's house, tell the children to stay put, dismount, and knock lightly on the back door. I can hear shuffling inside, but it takes a while for someone to open the door. Elizabeth's father opens the door a crack and when he sees it is me, he opens it wider.

"Josephine, what are you doing here at this hour?" he asks scanning the backyard nervously.

"Please, I need to speak to Elizabeth."

Elizabeth rushes to the door when she hears it is me.

"Are you okay? Is it your grandmother? What's the matter?"

"Please, if you'll let me speak. You told me that the word 'ami' is important and I never understood why you put so much emphasis on it, but I think I know why now. I heard that word tonight and I thought of you."

Her eyes go wide and she looks past me into the backyard. "Where?"

I breathe a sigh of relief. "I'll be right back," I say.

I race behind the shed where I left the children. I tell them to quickly follow me and we take off into the house. There is a trap door that I had never noticed before in the kitchen and Mrs. Julien shuffles them down the steps. I peek down and I see the children being engulfed by a woman, their mother! She has tears in her eyes as she looks up at me. My heart melts for them. In an instant, the trap door closes and Mr. and

Mrs. Julien turn to me. Mr. Julien grabs me by my shoulders "Josephine, you must tell no one what you did or saw here. Do you understand?"

"Yes, I understand."

"Get home quickly and be careful," Mrs. Julien instructs.

My heart pounds along with Buckeye's hooves as we race back home. I fall into bed but find it impossible to sleep. Too much is racing through my mind. *I just aided runaway slaves. What if someone finds out I helped them escape? What will happen to me?* I fret over this all night, tossing and turning until morning.

I make my way downstairs to breakfast and as my grandparents and I are dining on eggs, bacon, and biscuits, a knock comes at the door. My heart almost leaps out of my chest.

"Who could be calling at this early hour?" my grandfather asks curiously.

I hear Josiah answer the door, voices that I do not recognize, and then Josiah enters the dining room with a gentleman.

"Forgive me for interrupting and calling at this hour, but we had some runaways last night and I would like to ask if any of you fine folks heard or saw anything last night?"

"I'm mighty sorry to hear that, sir, but we did not hear or see anything last night. If we do, we will let you know," my grandfather replies, answering for all of us.

"And what about you, young lady?" the man questions while glaring at me.

My chest feels so tight and his glare is so steadfast that I almost can't get my words out.

"No, sir, I was asleep all night," I manage to lie.

After what seems like an eternity, he finally looks away.

"If no one saw or heard anything I must be on my way, but if you would please let us know if you happen upon any darkies. There was a female and her two young children as well as a couple of big bucks. I'd like to get them all back and make examples of them so that none of the others get any hankerings to run away. I'd like to find and have punished anyone who helped them run as well," he says while looking at me.

"We will be on the lookout for sure," my grandfather assures, causing the man to look away from me.

"Thank you, sir, good day."

The man leaves and I can finally breathe again.

"I never have liked that man," my grandmother says. "He mistreats his slaves, starving them and beating them to the brink of death. It's a wonder he is able to keep any of them healthy enough to get any work done."

"Who is he?" I ask.

"That is Frederick's father, Peter York."

No wonder he kept glaring at me. I can see where his son gets it. I say a silent prayer that the slaves make it all the way to freedom.

I remain jittery the rest of the day, but no one else came to the house and the days turn into weeks and there is no more mention of the runaways at all. It seems that everyone has forgotten about them, except for me. I can't help but remember how scared and hopeless the children were and then how relieved and happy they and their mother were when they were brought back together safely. It filled my heart with joy. I want to help more slaves escape, but I don't know how. It isn't likely I will stumble upon too many runaways in the bushes that I can lead to safety. I want to talk to Elizabeth and find out what I can do to help, but the last few times I have seen her we have been at various social gatherings and I definitely can't talk to her about such matters at those events. Hopefully I will be able to catch her alone soon. I have so many questions that need answers.

Chapter 18

It is a chilly day in November and I can't wait for school to let out, because my grandmother is allowing me to have dinner at Elizabeth's house. Finally, this evening, I will get the chance to discuss the runaways! Mrs. Boudreaux dismisses us and I lock arms with Elizabeth as we walk through the streets of Natchez to her house. There are still a few more hours left for her parents' shop to be open, so we leave our books in her room and go downstairs to help out in the store. It is very busy as many people are buying fabric and silk for their holiday dresses. One customer even purchased one of Elizabeth's paintings as she perused through the shop. We chat with the customers as we stock the shelves with the newest shipment of merchandise and before I know it, it is time for dinner. I don't feel right talking about that night at the dinner table, so I wait until Elizabeth and I are sitting on her bed safely in her room.

"Elizabeth, I have been dying to talk to you about this since the night it happened. Please be honest and tell me about what you and your parents do, you know, after hours."

Elizabeth's eyes widen, "I can't talk about it to anyone. Mother and Father told me to never tell a soul. Do you know how much trouble we could be in if the wrong people ever found out?"

"Yes, I have an idea of what could happen," I respond thinking back on the atrocities I have seen happen to the slaves. "But I already know what you do. I just want to know more about it."

Elizabeth shakes her head and bites her bottom lip. "Ok, but you can't tell a soul of what I am about to tell you."

"I won't. I love you and your family too much. I would die if I caused something bad to happen to you. I will take this to my grave." I respond crossing my heart.

"My mother and father never have liked the thought of slavery, but since we live right in the heart of slave country, they just accept it and go on about their business, especially since the slave owners are our customers. One day, a woman and her slave came into the shop and the woman purchased all sorts of items. She ordered her slave to carry them to the buggy. The slave couldn't get all the items in one trip even though she tried so hard. My parents could hear the woman yelling at the young girl to hurry. When the young girl had to make a second trip, the woman started yelling louder and louder and telling the girl how useless she was. This made the girl so nervous that she tripped and fell on the cobblestones cutting her knee. My mother ran out to help the girl while my father finished carrying the items to the buggy. Once the woman and slave left, a young man walked into the store. As soon as he opened his mouth, my parents knew he was not from around here. He was from up north. He told them he saw the kindness that was shown to the slave girl and wanted to know if that was something they would like to continue to do on a larger scale. My parents listened to the man talk about the Underground Railroad and how safe houses were needed as holding places until it was safe for the slave to continue on in their journey. He talked to them about the dangers of being a part of the Underground Railroad, but how rewarding it was to be able to help people escape the bonds of slavery. He offered my parents time to think about it, but they said they didn't need any time. They already knew they wanted to help. It wasn't long before the first runaway came to our back door, scared and hungry. We had everything in place though and were able to shelter them for a couple of days before it was safe for them to move on. Sometimes they move on by foot and other times we box them up as cargo from our store and ship them north on the river. We have been doing it since I was a little girl."

I sit listening to Elizabeth's story and almost can't contain myself.

"I want to help," I blurt out.

Elizabeth looks at me puzzled.

"I want to help. Helping those children that day made me feel like I had a purpose in life. I don't belong on a plantation full of slaves. I feel like my job is to help them escape that life and find their full potential within society. They are not dumb, ignorant people. My friend Benjamin is every bit as smart as me. We were learning together until I was caught teaching him and was sent down here."

"I understand where you are coming from, but how are you going to help? You can't exactly harbor slaves at your grandparents house."

"No, but I can educate them about the Underground Railroad and help them escape in that way."

"You would help your own family's slaves escape?"

"In a heartbeat."

"You are an odd girl, Josephine."

"I'll take that as a compliment," I say smiling.

Over the next few weeks, I learn everything I can about the Underground Railroad from Elizabeth and her family. I write to my Aunt Diane and discuss everything with her. I receive a letter back with more useful information and her telling me to also be very careful and smart about who I speak with and where I speak with them.

I decide to start with the house slaves, mainly Delilah. I step out of the house during the night and go to the house slave's quarters. I am able to catch many of the house slaves before they head upstairs to the loft to go to sleep.

"What brings you out here tonight, little missy?" Alexander asks.

"I have something important to talk to you all about. It's the Underground Railroad."

"Child, I know all about the Underground Railroad. White folk promising freedom and black folk believing them," Delilah responds.

"But it is real, Delilah. You heard about those two young children and their mother that escaped from the York plantation?"

"Yes, every plantation from here to Canada probably heard about them."

"I helped them escape."

"You did what?" She half screams. The astonishment in her voice was undeniable.

"The children were outside. I heard them crying. I reunited them with their mother at the safe house. I know the Underground Railroad is real."

"The Underground Railroad is nothing but a way to keep

the white folks' hounds in shape," Alexander says.

"What do you mean? I don't understand why you would want to stay a slave when you can escape to freedom."

"Child," Delilah begins looking at me with a sad expression. "We all hear about the Underground Railroad and we all see slaves get excited and decide to take off on their path to freedom. 'We gonna make it and live our own lives the way we want to live,' they say. Then we hear the hounds a-baying as they run, chasing that scent. Next morning, we see them sorry slaves being dragged behind the horses and watch as the light goes out of their eyes when they're hanging from the oak tree. I don't want to be someone's slave any more than the next person, but I do want to stay alive to see my Ann again."

I sneak back to my room feeling defeated. *Don't get discouraged,* I remember my aunt writing, *many will not want to attempt an escape. Your job is not to force them to escape. You are only providing them the knowledge that they will need to stay safer along their journey if they do decide to try to escape to freedom.* This thought makes me feel better. I am an agent of the Underground Railroad. My goal is to connect as many slaves as I can to the knowledge of the Railroad, but nothing more, unless I am absolutely needed.

Christmas is just around the corner and I know this is going to be the perfect time to reach out and connect with slaves from other plantations. My grandparents and I have been invited to numerous parties and the first one is tonight. I am more excited than ever. I can surely spread the word of the Underground Railroad among the house staff. I decide I will steal away under the cover of night to where the slaves are holding their celebration. Delilah said the slaves enjoy the night out as much as white folks do, if not more.

The party is a normal party. Men and women dressed up in their best dresses and tuxedos, the men bragging about how well their crops turned out this year and the women talking about the latest fashion. Elizabeth and I find a quiet corner to discuss our plan for the night. She will be my lookout as I talk to the slaves. We are both so nervous and jittery that we can barely eat. After a few hours of mingling politely, which I dislike immensely, it is time to make our move. Neither one of us is very popular, so it isn't too difficult to steal away from the crowd. We slip out the back door and make our way to the house slave's quarters. That is where Delilah said all the slaves from other plantations congregate while waiting on their owners. I take a deep breath and walk in alone. Elizabeth stays outside as my watch. Instantly, all eyes are on me.

"Good evening everyone," I say shyly. I feel awkward looking at all the slaves in their simple attire as I stand there before them in my ball gown.

I clear my throat, "I am here to speak with you today about freedom and the Underground Railroad."

"Dis be a trap," one man announces as he stands up.

Others nod in agreement and attempt to leave.

Alexander speaks up, "You can leave if ya like, but if you want to escape to freedom with knowin' 'bout where you going and who be there to help ya, I say you stay and listen to the little missy. Of course, you can always go at it on your own, blind as a bat with no help, dat be up to you."

Those that stood to leave slowly sit back down.

"I am not telling any of you to escape. That is your own choice. The dangers are real out there and if you get caught, you will most likely be whipped and hung. I am only here to provide you knowledge so that if you do choose to escape, you will have help along the way."

I tell them everything I know, starting with the first safe house, the Julien house. Before leaving, I wish them all the best of luck and tell them I will be praying for them. I make my way back outside and Elizabeth and I scurry back into the house and begin mingling again as if we never left.

It is only a few days after the party when word spreads that a few slaves have escaped from a nearby plantation. Elizabeth tells me at school that they had stopped at her house and were shipped further north on the Mississippi River. I pray they make it to freedom.

Each and every party I am invited to, I make a point to spread the word about the Underground Railroad. It is a few days after each of these parties that a few more slaves escape. Sometimes they all escape from the same plantation and sometimes they escape on the same night from different plantations. Even if I don't catch word that there is an escape, I can always tell when someone takes refuge at the Julien house, because Elizabeth is tired, yet on high alert.

I walk into my grandparent's house through the front door and stop short when I hear Uncle Charles and a group of men, including Mr. York and Frederick discussing something in the parlor. I move in closer to the slightly open door and peek through the crack so I can see and hear better.

"There have been too many escapes recently and they seem to occur shortly after a gathering. There must be someone taking advantage of this time and encouraging the slaves to escape right under our very noses," one gentleman says.

I can feel my heart leap in my chest.

"But who would do that?" someone asks. "There hasn't been anyone new in town. All of the people I have seen at each of the parties are the people that we have known for years and who own slaves themselves."

"There is one person who we have not known for years," Frederick says with disgust.

"And who might you be speaking of?" my grandfather asks.

"Your very own granddaughter, Josephine," he says with disdain in his voice.

"Now you listen here young man! Don't you come into my house placing blame on my granddaughter. I don't know what you have against her, but she would never do anything like this!"

"My apologies, sir, but she did teach a negro to read, did she not?" asks Frederick.

I hold my breath as my grandfather hesitates.

"Yes, Frederick, she did teach a negro to read, but she was a child then and she has grown into a much more mature, young woman now. She would never do the things that you are suggesting."

"Forgive me, sir, but I don't agree. I feel she has a hand in this and I will definitely be keeping my eye on her," he says as he turns and looks towards the door. I move quickly, praying that he did not see me. I head towards my room as my heart pounds with every step.

Chapter 19

It's New Year's Eve and my grandparents and I are on our way to the neighbor's plantation for the last holiday party of the year. It is always a big one: the Dubois' love bringing in the New Year and go all out with their meal and festivities.

We arrive and I help my grandmother to her seat and then excuse myself to find Elizabeth. I make my way through the crowd of men and women dressed in their best attire. Some bid me good evening while others just ignore me. I find Elizabeth in a corner of the parlor seated with her mother and father, sipping tea. She jumps up as soon as she sees me and runs over and gives me a hug. We start chattering like two hens in a hen house, because after all, it has been a whole day since we have seen each other. As we sit discussing our day, I keep feeling as if I am being watched. I look around the room only to lock eyes with Frederick. It appears he was serious when he said he was going to be keeping his eye on me. This is definitely going to make things more difficult.

The meal is served and it is absolutely delicious. The list is endless - glazed ham, sweet potatoes, mashed potatoes, corn, biscuits, green beans, and carrots. Everything is rounded out with the most delicious cakes and pies for dessert. I try to eat like a lady, but it is hard because everything is so good. I wish Millie hadn't tightened my corset so tight, I can barely breathe at this point. The music in the ballroom begins to play and we all venture there to finish out the night with dancing. Elizabeth and I have other plans though. Once it appears that everyone is engrossed in their own affairs, we head towards the back door. I glance around the room quickly to take in Frederick's whereabouts. He is across the room, facing the other direction, thank goodness.

We walk quickly down the hall and just as we begin to open the back door, I hear a voice that I have grown to hate.

"And where might you two ladies be going?" Frederick asks as a couple of other boys from school gather behind him.

"We were just going out to get some air," I respond quickly.

"Why would you go out the back way? The back of the house is mostly for the slaves, not for fine, upstanding, young ladies such as yourselves," he mocks.

"I felt faint and this was the quickest way out," I reply.

"Well that's funny."

"What is so funny about that?" I demand.

"You haven't made it outside to get some much-needed fresh air, yet here you are standing strong as ever. That is what I admire about you Josephine. You are a very strong, young woman. I like that. We could be a powerful couple one day, you and I. There is only one thing that gets in the way."

"What's that?" I ask. "The fact that I despise you?"

One of the young men in his group snickers, but stops quickly as soon as Frederick glares at him.

"No, it's the fact that you are a thief."

"What? I have never stolen anything in my life," I say genuinely confused.

"You have been providing the darkies with pertinent information needed to help them escape our plantations. To me, that is the same as you physically stealing them away in the night."

"I have done nothing of the sort and never will. I merely need some fresh air and I need it even more now that you have accused me of such nonsense. Now, if you will please excuse Elizabeth and me, we will be on our way."

I turn for the door, but before I can make a move, Frederick grabs my arm pulling me towards him and whispers quietly in my ear, "I know what you are doing and I suggest you stop or—"

"I have done nothing and I recommend you never touch me again," I say jerking my arm away.

I storm outside where Elizabeth is waiting for me. My whole body is shaking. "Oh, how much I despise that boy!" I shout.

I fume outside for a while, but Elizabeth is able to calm me down enough to go back in for the remainder of the party.

I sit in my room that night looking at the stars while holding my cornhusk doll. I feel like a failure. I did not talk to any of the slaves for fear that Frederick would still be watching me. The only thing keeping me from quitting is remembering what my aunt said about being smart when I spread the information: Anything done at the wrong time or place could put myself and others in danger. I did the wise thing. I did not fail. My eyes grow heavy as I start to think about Benjamin. I wish I was home and looking at the stars with him. I miss him so much. I still need to figure out how to get him, his mother, and grandmother together again. I say a quick prayer asking God to help me make this happen.

It's a beautiful sunny New Year's Day and I am enjoying the mild, winter weather outside. I hear the footsteps of a horse coming up the lane and normally I would not be alarmed by this, but I can tell this horse is at an all-out gallop. I hurry around the house to see who it is. I can tell by the blonde hair that it is Elizabeth. She hops off the horse before it even comes to a complete stop and runs to me.

"Josephine, Josephine! It was horrible! They came in and destroyed so much stuff. I have never been so scared in my life!"

I grab her by the shoulders. "What are you talking about? What happened? Who destroyed what?"

"We can't talk here," she whispers looking around with wide eyes.

She pulls me by my arm and we take off down the dirt path. We walk around behind the house slaves' quarters to a little clump of trees. She looks around for a minute and then begins her story.

"My family and I had just made it home after the party. I was in my room saying my prayers and I heard the sound of breaking glass and my mother scream. I was scared, but I ran downstairs anyway to see what was going on. There were men that I had never seen before. They came in and started smashing things and saying 'Where are they?' and 'We know you are hiding slaves in here!' My father told me to go to my room and I obeyed, but I could hear things breaking and my father saying that we were hiding no one. It felt like an eternity, but they finally left. I went back downstairs. There was broken furniture and dishes everywhere, but my parents were not harmed, thank goodness."

"They didn't find anything, did they?"

"No. If they had, no telling what would have happened to me and my family. They said they would be keeping an eye on us and that we better not be helping slaves escape or else."

"Frederick," I say as I kick a stone. "He sent those men to your house."

"Do you really think so?"

"He caught us on the way out of that party. He knows what we do but has no proof. He was trying to find proof last night by following us and then raiding your house. He probably never thought you would be in on anything until he saw us both leaving the party last night. We will have to lay low for a while."

"That's another reason why I had to come here."

"Why?"

"Because my parents think it is too dangerous for me to stay here now that people seem to be catching on to what we do. I am to leave for France and live with my grandmother as soon as possible. My parents are sending a letter to her today to make the arrangements."

This news hits me like a ton of bricks. Why do the people I love keep getting taken away from me? Tears start to well up in my eyes.

"You are going to be leaving?"

"Please don't cry. You'll make me cry. I don't want to leave you or my parents, but I don't want to live in fear either. Last night was scary!"

I don't know what to say, so I just continue to try to keep the tears from overflowing.

"My mother says that I will have more access to the arts in France, so that is exciting."

I grab Elizabeth and hug her tightly.

"I am going to miss you terribly, but I want you to be safe and I want you to conquer the world with your art. You are an amazing artist and you deserve this opportunity. I am going to cry, though. I can't help it."

We both hold each other tightly and cry.

After a few minutes, I push Elizabeth back slightly and look into her eyes, all red and swollen from crying.

"That is enough of this nonsense. We are strong, young, southern women. We will make it through this and we will be stronger because of it."

Elizabeth bursts out laughing, "You sound like your grandmother!"

"Oh, my goodness, I do!" I agree, breaking into delirious laughter.

We laugh and cry until we are exhausted. We finally compose ourselves and Elizabeth heads back home and I go inside to join my grandparents for dinner.

My grandparents are a bit solemn during the meal and I can't quite figure out why, until I am about to excuse myself.

"I heard some men ransacked the Julien home. Is that why Elizabeth was here, to tell you about it?" my grandmother asks.

"Yes, how did you find out?"

"I heard it from your Uncle Charles just a bit ago. He heard about it while he was in town," my grandfather explains.

"I forbid you to see that girl again," Grandmother blurts out.

I am taken back. "What? Why?"

"I cannot have you associating with someone like that. It will give you a bad name."

"But no evidence was found that they do what those men claim."

"I do not care. You will no longer associate with that girl or her family, do you understand?"

"No, I don't understand! She and her parents are my friends! You will not tell me who I can and cannot be friends with!"

"Young lady! You do not talk to your grandmother that way!" my grandfather yells.

I stand up quickly. "Grandmother, Grandfather, I love you both, but I cannot allow you to control me. I have my own life and I need to live it my way." I turn and head for my room.

I hear my grandmother yelling at me as I climb the stairs, but I cannot make out any words. I slam the door of my room and throw myself on the bed, praying that I would get to go home soon. I don't want to live one more minute in Natchez, Mississippi, especially not without Elizabeth.

Chapter 20

"Josephine, Josephine, wake up child."

As my eyes flutter open, I can't help but think about how odd it is for Delilah to be waking me up. I usually wake up on my own or Millie wakes me up, but I don't even have school today.

"Good morning, Delilah, this is a pleasant surprise—" I stop when I notice that Delilah has tears streaming down her face. "What's the matter?"

"It's your grandmother, child. She went to be with Jesus sometime in the night."

I don't know what to say or do. I feel like I have been punched in the stomach. The last words I said to my grandmother were words of defiance. Tears came to my eyes.

"It's my fault she is dead."

"What are you talking about, child?"

"I caused her to get angry with me. It is my fault she is dead. If I had just agreed to do what she asked instead of being stubborn then she would still be alive."

"It's definitely not your fault, so get that out of your little head! Your grandmother's health has been ailing for a while now. She was talking to me the other day about how tired she was. You saw how thin she was getting. It is her time to be with Jesus now. Even if you hadn't disagreed with her, Jesus still would have come last night to welcome her into heaven."

I nod, trying to believe her as she helps me get dressed.

I make my way into my grandmother's room where she is still lying in bed. She looks so peaceful. My grandfather gets up from his chair and engulfs me in a big hug.

"She loved you so much, Josephine," he says. "You reminded her so much of your mother Charlotte. Every night she would tell me that you were a good, strong girl and will grow up to be a good, strong woman. Even last night after the disagreement we had, she said the same thing. She liked your determination and willingness to stand up for what you believed in even though it went against our wishes. She loved you with all her heart, Josephine. Never forget that."

"I won't, Grandfather, I won't," I manage to say in between sobs.

The next few days are a blur. People come from all over Natchez and neighboring towns to pay respects to my grandmother. We lay her to rest in the family cemetery just outside the garden, next to the magnolia tree. It's a chilly, winter day and I am numb, not from the cold but from the fact that I have never been to a funeral of a loved one before. It is the oddest feeling to know that I will never be able to talk to my grandmother again or feel her warmth as she gives me a hug followed by a kiss on the cheek. It's these thoughts that keep swirling in my head and keep the tears welling in my eyes.

Once my grandmother has been placed in her final resting place and everyone has left, my grandfather taps on my bedroom door.

"May I come in?" he asks.

"Of course," I say continuing to stare out the window.

"I have been thinking. Since your grandmother passed away and no longer needs your assistance, you may go home if you would like. I am still able to get out and about and work every day and I am afraid you will get lonely in this house by yourself. I will miss you terribly, but I want you to be happy."

I can't believe it. I am going to go home!

"I am going to miss you as well, Grandfather, but I would very much like to go home."

"I will get your trip squared away then."

He turns to leave the room, but stops once he reaches the door and turns around.

"Oh, I almost forgot. Your grandmother left you Delilah in her will, so she will be in your possession on your trip home." At that, he turns and leaves.

I sit on the window seat, amazed. I can't believe it. Prayers do come true! I am getting to return home and take Delilah with me. I say a quick prayer thanking God before rushing around in search of Delilah. I finally find her standing just outside of the slave quarters.

"Delilah!" I scream as I run towards her.

She looks at me with wide eyes, "What, child, what has happened now?"

"I get to go back home!"

"That's great, I am happy for you."

"And you know the best part?" I press beaming ear to ear.

"No, child, what?"

"You're coming with me."

"Don't mess with me, child."

"I'm not. Grandmother left you to me in her will. Where I go, you go, and that means back to Kentucky to be with your daughter and grandson."

With that news, she lifts her hands. "Prays Jesus," she screams. "I knew you were my ticket back to my Ann. Bless you, child, bless you!" She hugs me so tightly I worry that my eyes will pop right out of their sockets.

I go to bed that night with mixed emotions. I am still saddened over the death of my grandmother, but happy that I will be going home soon and taking Delilah with me. *What a surprise for Ann!* I kiss my cornhusk doll goodnight and roll over to let sleep overcome me.

Chapter 21

It takes a couple of weeks to get myself packed and my trip planned. I watch through teary eyes as Elizabeth embarks on her journey to France. We promise each other we will write every day.

Finally, it is my turn to embark on my journey home. I say my goodbyes to everyone. I feel sad having to leave Alexander, my grandfather, my Aunt Theresa and Uncle Charles behind, but I am overcome by my happiness of going home and taking Delilah with me. I am almost jumping for joy as Alexander pulls up with the buggy. The ride to the port is uneventful with the exception of passing Frederick. He sneers at me as we ride by. I pray I never have to lay eyes on him again.

Millie, Delilah, and I board the ship and I wave from the deck as we embark. I watch as we round the bend and Natchez disappears from site. Although it was never home, I learned so much during my stay. Unlike what my mother wished, it did not make me want to live her life. Instead, it strengthened what was already within me and allowed me to begin to help those suffering in the bonds of slavery. *My mother wants a strong woman. She is going to get one.*

The closer we get to home, the colder it gets. Big chunks of ice float along in the river and the snow falls thick from the sky. We dock at Maysville and my heart sinks. There is no way we are going to get home. The roads are virtually impassable in town. We will never be able to travel by carriage all the way to the country. I look around, wondering what to do. Millie and Delilah are looking to me for guidance. Thankfully, I only brought one trunk home for easier travels. My father will pick up everything I left behind on one of his trips to Natchez in the spring. I pull my cape around me a little tighter and tell Millie and Delilah that we will have to walk to my grandmother's house and that hopefully someone will know to look for us there when they make it through the snow. I reach down to grab one end of my trunk but as I do, someone's hand touches mine.

"Let me get that for you, ma'am."

I look up quickly. "Benjamin!"

He looks so different. His voice is deeper and he is much taller, but he still has the same cheerful smile.

If we weren't in public, I would throw my arms around him. I am so happy to see him.

"How did you get here? Aren't the roads impassable?"

"I brought the sled and lots of blankets. It should fit everyone very well. Your father told me to take you to your grandmother's house and then we could embark on our journey home tomorrow. Hopefully this icy snow will have let up by then."

Benjamin grabs the trunk and slides it onto the sled and then helps me in. Delilah climbs in next to me and we snuggle under the warm blankets. Millie, on the other hand, climbs in next to Benjamin in the driver's seat, which I think is odd. I figured she would want to sit under all the blankets in the back where it is warmer. I quickly realize why she sat with

Benjamin. She starts talking to him and touching him.

Delilah nudges me and whispers, "I told you she was a flirt. She had all the boys eating out of the palm of her hand in Natchez. That girl will never be happy though, it seems she always wants what someone else has."

I had no idea she was like this. I hadn't really paid that much attention to her in Natchez, because I blamed her for getting me sent down there and because she was always so mean to me. She has my attention now though and it appears she has Benjamin's as well.

My grandmother is so happy to see me again, as I am her. We have a big meal and then talk most of the night. By morning, the sun is up glistening off all the snow. It is so bright and beautiful. I once again snuggle in with Delilah amongst all the blankets. Millie seats herself up front with Benjamin again, which aggravates me a bit, but for what reason I do not know. I push that feeling away and take in all the beautiful snow-covered scenery as Shadow pulls us home.

My father, mother, John, and Aunt Diane are all on the front porch when we pull up. My father helps me out of the sled and engulfs me in a huge hug, followed by my mother and John. He has changed so much as well. He is almost taller than our father! Last came Diane. It is so hard to hold in my excitement over being home. I turn to tell my mother about Delilah, but Benjamin had already taken her and Millie around back to the slave quarters.

"Where is Ann?" I ask mother.

"Does it matter, dear?"

"Yes, I want to see her."

"She best be in the house tending to her duties. I thought sending you to live with your grandmother would have put a

163

stop to your fascination with the slaves. I guess she became soft in her old age. How was her funeral? Did father surround her with magnolias like she wanted? I wish I could have been there, but these Kentucky winters seem to get worse every year."

"Grandmother's funeral was nice and she taught me well. When she passed, she left me one of her slaves. I was merely going to tell Ann so she could help her get settled and start her into the housework. Heaven forbid a slave have the sense to get started on their own."

Mother smiles, "So you have changed. Please, go tend to what belongs to you."

As I walk into the house to find Ann, I hear Mother say to Father, "She is growing into a fine woman."

I find Ann in my room getting everything ready for my return. She must have heard me walk into the room, because she turns around so quickly it startles me.

"Josephine!" She hugs me so tightly. "My you have grown. You look so—"

"There is someone that I would like you to see," I cut her off excitedly. "Come on." I grab her arm and start pulling her through the house and outside to the slave quarters behind the house.

"Goodness, Josephine, you almost pulled my arm off," she says as we walk inside. "What could possibly be so important?"

"Ann?"

Ann gasps as she spots the woman across the room. "Momma? Momma, is that really you?"

"Yes, baby, it's me," Delilah answers, eyes glistening.

"How did you...how are you here?"

Delilah nods towards me. "I belong to Josephine now. She

brought me back to you."

"Thank you, Josephine, thank you," Ann cries.

"Don't thank me, I didn't do anything special. You two catch up. I will have Millie help me unpack."

I swing by the stable to find Benjamin tending to Shadow. I run up and hug him from behind.

"I missed you so much! Thank you for taking care of Shadow while I was away. She looks good."

He moves me back so he can look at me. A smile spreads across his face. "I was afraid you would have changed living with your grandmother."

"I'll be honest, I did falter in the beginning. I almost fell in line with my family, but I met someone who helped me follow my heart. You should get to know her better too. She's in the quarters with your mother now." With that I leave him and head for the house.

It is so good being back home. I fall right back into my old routine like I never left. Lessons are so much more fun and relaxing with John and my Aunt Diane. John knows that my aunt and I have different views from him, but he loves us anyway. We often discuss the issue of slavery and each of us listens to the others thoughts and comments. Although we never change our views, we are determined to not let that get in the way of our love for each other and John never dares tell my parents that I am the same old Josephine. He says the hardest years of his life so far were the ones spent without seeing my smiling face every day. I agree - life is better when I am home.

Chapter 22

Before I know it, summer has arrived, hot and dry. The drought has taken a toll on our crops and the heat has made us all cranky. To make things even worse, John has decided to go to college. He is going to attend Transylvania University in Lexington to study business in order to help my father in growing the family farm. The plan is for him to accompany Aunt Diane to Maysville, stay at my grandmother's house for a few days, and then make the journey to Lexington. My mother is very nervous for him to travel that far alone, so she has made him promise to write as soon as he arrives in Lexington.

The day he leaves is difficult for everyone, but especially me. I no sooner come back home and start to enjoy his company when he decides to leave. Father is sad, but I can tell he is trying to hold it back and be strong for John. Mother follows John around all morning continually asking him if he has everything and keeps reminding him to write as soon as he arrives in Lexington.

I watch as his trunk is loaded and hug him and Diane through teary eyes before they climb into the buggy. I wave my handkerchief until the buggy is out of sight. Now I have the task of keeping my mother calm until we hear from John.

The days go by and my mother becomes more and more of a

nervous wreck. She keeps wondering why John's letter has not made it yet. She sends Benjamin to the post office every day to check for his letter. Father and I keep trying to reassure her that everything is okay and his letter will arrive soon. Finally, Benjamin comes trotting up to the front porch on Shadow, holding a letter. Mother, Father, and I are enjoying the cool, evening breeze, so I quickly leave my seat to retrieve the letter from Benjamin and read it aloud:

Dear Mother, Father, and of course, Josephine,

I made it safely to Lexington. Transylvania is very nice and I have already met many new friends. If you have not heard yet, there was an explosion in Maysville while I was staying with Grandmother. It happened on a Sunday night whilst everyone was sleeping. Everyone at Grandmother's house is alright, it just rattled the windows and made the clock stop at five minutes before two o'clock. Other people were not so lucky. Aunt Diane and I ran out of the house to see what happened, as did most others. We heard that five men discharged over 27,000 pounds of gunpowder on the west end in Maysville. We made our way to where the magazine exploded and began aiding individuals who had been hurt by the blast. Some 33 houses had been demolished with others suffering broken windows and chimneys. Diane and I began working together removing people from the rubble and tending to their various injuries. There were large stones everywhere. Someone even said that a stone weighing 102 pounds was blown completely across the Ohio River into Aberdeen! It is only by divine intervention that no one was killed. It is still hard for me to believe after witnessing the destruction.

I must tell you, though, and I hope you will not be angry with me, but after being in that situation and being able to help those people in need, I feel I have found my true calling in life. I no longer wish to study business, so I will be studying medicine here at Transylvania. I wish to become a doctor.

Yours truly,

John

This news is a shock to all of us. Father isn't too happy, but Mother and I want John to be happy, so if helping others makes him happy then that is good enough for us. I race to my room immediately to write to John and tell him how happy I am for him that he has found his path and that I will support him in any way that I can.

Chapter 23

"Millie, where did the time go?" I ask after waking up one morning in October. "It seems like yesterday we finally returned home, yet here it is, fall already, and not just any fall day, it's the first day of the fair!"

"It goes where it goes. Just another day for me. Nothing ever changes."

I am not going to let Millie get me down with her negative views on life, not today. *Today and tomorrow are different.*

"We are going to be attending our first fair and it is right here in Germantown. Aren't you excited, Millie?"

"It's going to be hot and muggy," she spits as she goes around opening the windows, "and I's just going to be tending to your every need."

She is right. I can't argue with that, so I don't say another word. I'm not going to allow this day to be spoiled though. Family and friends are staying at our house to be closer to the festivities, so these next few days are going to be full of laughter, fun, and parties.

I hop out of bed to get dressed. Mary will be here soon. She is going to ride with us today. I can't wait. I heed Millie's warning about it being hot and dusty and pick a light blue dress. She helps lace me up, tying it so tightly that I can't breathe.

"Millie, will you loosen the laces a bit? I feel I'm going to pass out already."

"Yes ma'am."

She pulls them even tighter. I turn and glare at her. A part of me wants to slap her, but I refrain. I would probably do the same if I was in her position. I turn back around.

"Loosen them, please," I say in a firmer tone. Thankfully she does. One notch tighter and I feel I would have passed out for sure!

I descend the steps just as there is a knock at the door. I open it myself to find Mary standing on the other side in a light-yellow dress.

"Mary, you look so beautiful!"

"As do you, Jo."

"Come on, let's find everyone else so we can go," I say as I grab her hand.

We find everyone in the dining room enjoying a huge breakfast of grits, eggs, biscuits, gravy, and bacon.

"Good morning, Jo. Good morning, Mary," my mother greets us with a smile. "Please have a seat and get something to eat."

"Thank you, but I ate at home," Mary politely refuses.

"I can't eat anything, I'm too excited," I say.

"Nonsense, little missy. Now you sit right down and eat. You so skinny a strong wind will blow you over. Now eat you some eggs and biscuits. I made the grits just the way you like 'em, with a lot of butter," Frannie commands as she ushers me into a seat.

"And you Miss Mary, you could use some more meat on them bones. You sit right down here next to Josephine and I'll make you a plate."

It's hard to say no to Frannie because she sure can cook, so we sit and eat enough to please her until finally we are off. It is a beautiful October day. The rains from the previous days have brought a crispness to the air, but the sun is shining down from the brilliant, blue sky. Shadow is pulling our buggy and I can't help but notice that Benjamin is dressed in his best suit sitting straight and tall holding the reigns. No one really knows what to expect, but we are ready to find out.

The Currens' property, where the fair is being held, is not far from ours and it isn't long before we are pulling up alongside the other buggies that have already arrived at the fair. There are large oak trees all around and the grounds are enclosed by a post and rail fence. We make our way to the entrance and we each hand our ten cents to the gentleman at the entrance who in return gives us a blue ribbon. The gentlemen tie their ribbons in their buttonholes while Mary and I tie ours around our wrists.

I can feel the excitement in the air as we enter the grounds. Men and women of all ages mingle. It isn't long before Mr. Stevenson, the editor of the Maysville Eagle, opens the fair with an address. Once he is finished, the band begins to play and Mary and I take off to see what we can find. There are various contests being held throughout the grounds. We watch as boys vie to be crowned as the best rider and as ladies wait nervously to see if their pie is voted the best. Then it is my turn to wait nervously. Father has entered several of our draft horses and they are in the ring showing. I watch as each horse is taken around the ring and as the judges look them over one by one. It feels like an eternity, but finally one of our horses takes best of show! Exhilarated, we head for the shade of the oak trees to treat ourselves to a delicious, victory meal. White linens are laid out everywhere as many sit to eat and talk about the events they have witnessed thus far.

"Josephine, did you happen to see that George was here?" Mother asks.

"Yes, Mother, I saw George."

"Did you speak to him?"

"No, Mother, I did not speak to him. He was all the way across the show ring. Would you have liked me to holler at him?"

"Don't be ridiculous, Josephine, young ladies don't holler. I do think you should find a way to speak to him today, though. I hear he has eyes for you and he comes from a good family. He would be a good match for you."

I can hear Mary snickering. She knows I have no interest in finding a beau despite my mother always pushing the fact.

Not wanting to start an argument, I agree to speak to him. I never said how long, though, so I figure a passing 'good day' will be sufficient.

The meal is delicious and is topped off with Frannie's apple pie. Every bite floods my mouth with the delicious mixture of sweet apples and cinnamon spice. Her pie would surely have won first prize had she been allowed to enter.

After the meal, Mary and I excuse ourselves to do some more exploring. We wind our way through the crowd of people before stopping to watch the sheep show. They look like little puffs of cotton bouncing around in the ring. I am enjoying myself immensely when I feel a tap on my shoulder. I turn around and come face to face with George. Mary snickers and I shoot her a look that immediately wipes the smile off her face.

"Hello, Josephine, how are you?" he asks.

"I'm fine, thank you," I reply turning back around, hoping he gets the hint and leaves. He doesn't.

"May I accompany you home this evening?"

I start to form the word no, but then I happen to glance across the ring and catch sight of Benjamin. He is smiling and laughing. Millie is with him, as well as a couple of other slave girls that I have caught glimpses of at various parties. They seem to be having a good time. Millie and one of the other girls can't seem to keep their hands off of Benjamin. They keep touching his arms and shoulders and Millie leans in and kisses Benjamin on the cheek. This sight makes me suddenly nauseous and I reach out and grasp the railing and take a couple of deep breaths. I quickly regain composure hoping that no one has noticed.

"Josephine, did you hear me? I would like to accompany you home this evening," George repeats.

I turn to him, "Yes, George, I would very much like for you to accompany me."

Mary looks at me bewildered, but I turn my attention back to Benjamin and squeeze the fence rail tighter.

George continues to attempt to make conversation and I answer his questions politely, but my mind is elsewhere.

Why does seeing Benjamin with Millie and those other girls have such an effect on me? He is my friend and I want him to be happy. Of course, he is going to want to have a family, but I just didn't think it would be so soon. I want to keep him as my friend, because once he finds a wife, he is going to tell her all his hopes and dreams and not me. That's what it is – I am just afraid of losing his friendship.

The grand champion sheep is crowned ending the day's events. Mary, George, and I walk to the carriages. Mary keeps giving me sideways looks until finally she leans in and whispers, "What changed your mind?"

I shake my head and shrug, "I don't know. Maybe having a beau won't be so bad," I lie.

We climb into one of my carriages because we have to take Mary home and George's carriage is too full with his family. He will accompany me and then walk home. He says he doesn't mind walking because it is a beautiful evening and spending time with me makes the walk home worth it.

Our carriage is hooked to Shadow and being driven by Old Tom. Part of me did this to keep Millie from sitting up front with Benjamin, who is driving the other buggy. I didn't want to have to watch her as she pawed at him on the ride home. It was like she could read my mind, because she glared at me as she climbed in next to Old Tom.

"Giddy up," Tom says.

The carriage lurches forward as Shadow begins to trot home.

The evening quiet is disturbed by a loud bang.

Millie screams as Shadow rears up and takes off at breakneck speed. Mary and I grab each other as the scenery whips by and I can hear George cursing. It feels like an eternity, but in reality, it isn't very long at all before Tom regains control of Shadow.

"Easy girl," I hear Tom say, "it was just one of dem ole firecrackers. We okay now girl. Let's trot on home."

The rest of the trip home is uneventful. Mary and I chit chat along the way. George doesn't say a word, but I can see the tension in his eyes and on his face. We drop Mary off at her house, and shortly after, we are crossing the two ponds with my house in view. Tom stops in front of the house and I start to get out, but George doesn't move.

"I'm going to have a few words with your boy in the stable, Josephine."

I don't know what he has planned, but I know it isn't going to be good.

"I'll ride around to the back as well," I say. "If you're upset about Shadow getting spooked, there's no need to worry about that. We all came out of it okay."

"It should not have happened and he needs to learn to keep control of the horse," he responds.

My heart quickens as we near the stable. We pull in and Millie disappears into the house quickly through the back way. Benjamin is still in the stable putting things away and getting Storm settled into her stall. As Tom begins unhooking Shadow, George hops off the buggy and grabs the horsewhip, starting to beat both Tom and Shadow before I can stop him. Shadow starts to jump around in fear and Old Tom cries out in pain. Benjamin looks on in horror, as do I. I exit the buggy as quickly as possible in my big hoops and grab George's arm.

"Stop! Stop this right now! I will not have you beating my horse or my slave!"

"They almost got us hurt! They both need to learn their lesson!"

"But we are fine, so let it go and leave my property now! I never want to see you again!"

"You are going to choose the beasts over me?"

"I am choosing kindness and loyalty over you. You are nothing but a bully and I will not associate with anyone who mistreats people the way you do!"

"I do not see a person here, just a dumb horse and slave."

"Regardless of what you see they are both my property and I will not have you harm them in any way."

"Everyone said you were a negro lover. I didn't believe it until now. Choosing an ignorant slave over me, that's absurd. I will tell everyone how you are and you will grow up and become an old maid, a disgrace to your family name," he shouts as he storms out, leaving me to tend to Tom and Shadow's wounds. Luckily neither is hurt badly.

"Tom, I'm so sorry," I say trying to comfort him.

"It's not your fault, little missy. I should have kept better control of this here mare."

"What happened?" Benjamin asks as he gently strokes Shadow's muzzle to calm her down.

I tell him as he calms Shadow and checks her for wounds.

"I'm glad you stepped in, because I was about to take matters into my own hands. The way white people treat us is no better than animals," he grumbles punching one hand with the other. "This life is not fair. I have so much more to offer than to be someone's slave."

"Hush boy!" Tom pipes up quickly. "Talk like that get us both killed."

Benjamin looks away, anger clearly spreading across his face. He turns his attention back to Shadow and his face softens as he removes her bridle and speaks softly to her.

"I must go back to the house. They will be wondering where I am."

Benjamin grabs my arm, "Thank you again for protecting Tom and Shadow." Before I can turn to leave, he pulls me into a quick hug. I want to melt in that warm embrace forever, but as soon as it begins, it ends. I exit the stable quickly.

As I am leaving, I hear Tom say, "That right there will get you hung quicker than anything. Hugging a white girl. Boy, you ain't right in da head."

176

I head to my room to get ready for bed. We have another long day ahead of us tomorrow and I am exhausted, but for some reason sleep does not come quickly. I can still feel Benjamin's arms around me and although I know it isn't right, I want more. I remove the cornhusk doll he made for me four years ago from its hiding place, hold it tightly, and finally drift off to sleep.

Chapter 24

"I can't believe it, Mother. Five years have passed and John has completed his medical classes at Transylvania, completed an apprenticeship in Lexington, and now is going to be coming home to open his own practice in Augusta. I have missed him so much! I can't wait for him to be close by again."

"He has accomplished quite a bit in the past five years. I am very proud of him. I know he is a man and I no longer have to worry about him, he has found his path. I am; however, concerned about you Jo."

"You're concerned about me? Why?"

"Many of the girls your age have found beaus or are married now. There has not been a single gentleman caller to see you."

"Good grief, Mother, not this again. I am not interested in getting married at this time. I feel that -"

"At this time, at this time? Josephine! If you wait too much longer all the good men will be taken and you will be left with what is left, or worse, you will end up like your Aunt Diane and be an old maid!"

"That will be fine with me. She seems happy enough and she gets to come and go as she pleases," I say shrugging my shoulders.

"That's absurd! No woman ever wants to be an old maid.

You just wait until your father hears about this talk."

"Hears what?" Father asks as he enters the dining room to take his place at the table for supper.

"That your daughter is not interested in marriage at this time! She is going to end up like your sister if she's not careful."

"Well now, Diane does seem happy and comes and goes as she pleases," he replies with a smile and a wink.

Mother glares at him, "This is not a joking matter."

"Yes ma'am. I'm sorry," he apologizes stifling laughter.

"I'm serious. What have you heard from some of the men around town? Is no one interested in our daughter? Is there something wrong with her?"

"For goodness sake, Mother, I'm sitting right here."

"I have heard some talk. There are some boys interested, but they are afraid.

"Afraid of what?" Mother demands.

"They say she is too strong willed and has an air about her that makes them too nervous to even approach."

I snicker.

"What are you laughing at? This is not a bit funny," Mother snaps.

"It's your fault, Mother."

"My fault, what do you mean my fault?"

"You made me this way. You wanted a good, strong, southern woman. Well, here she is."

My father starts to chuckle. "She does have a point, Charlotte."

"Well, can you tone it down some? Be a little meeker when you are around the young gentlemen?"

"Yes, Mother, I will try," I say not wanting to argue over something as silly as men. *I guess there would be no harm in taking on a caller or two just to please her.*

"Well, now that the important item of the day is out of the way," my father begins chuckling, "I heard some disturbing news today."

"What news is that?" I ask.

"A white man named John Brown, with a band of twenty-one men, raided an arsenal at Harpers Ferry, Virginia. They caught him, though."

"What is so disturbing about that? You said they caught him," Mother inquires.

"Yes, Charlotte, but those men were raiding that arsenal to retrieve guns to arm slaves."

"What? Why would anyone want to do something as ignorant as arm slaves? Don't they know they are dumb animals? They would shoot us all!"

"That's the point, Mother. These people don't want to be our slaves. They want their own lives and there are people out there who are listening to their cries and taking action."

"That is absurd."

"She's right, Charlotte, and it seems like the rift between those of us that want to keep slavery and those that want to abolish it is becoming larger."

"Those northerners need to keep their noses out of our business down here," Mother says, disgusted.

My thoughts drift off as my mother and father discuss other happenings of the day.

Maybe slavery really will be abolished one day and Benjamin and his mother and grandmother can come and go as they please and never have to worry about being separated again. I can't wait to tell Benjamin the news this evening during our study session. Thankfully, nobody has found out that after returning home all those years ago I had picked up with teaching Benjamin right where I left off. Our study sessions have turned into more of discussing current events as opposed to traditional studies, and this is the perfect type of material to discuss.

After everyone has retired to bed, I slip out of my room and tiptoe quietly down the stairs and out the door, headed for the stable. There is a cold nip in the air this October evening, so I pull my shawl tighter around my shoulders and hurry quickly to the barn where Benjamin and I had decided to meet this evening. I slip through the barn door and close it quickly behind me to keep the chill out. I breathe in deeply, taking in the scents of the hay and horses. Shadow whinnies quietly, so I go to her. She sticks her nose out from the stall and I run my hand across her soft muzzle.

"Sorry, girl, I should have brought you an apple."

There is a noise behind me. I turn around quickly just in time to have a handful of hay thrown in my face.

"Benjamin, what was that for?" I ask as I grab up a handful of hay and throw it back at him.

I duck and move as more hay comes my way. The next thing I know, Benjamin's arms are around me and we tumble to the ground laughing. I can feel each muscle in his arms, and as I look into his eyes, I feel a warmth rush through my body like I've never felt before.

A loud crash breaks our reverie.

We both jump up quickly. My heart is pounding out of my chest as I look around to see what made the noise.

"It's okay, Shadow knocked over her feed bucket," Benjamin says with a sigh of relief.

We take another quick look around the barn and then find a

warm spot to discuss everything that has occurred since our last meeting. I tell him the news about John Brown.

"Don't ever give up hope. More and more people are speaking out against the evils of slavery."

"One day, I will be a free man. I can feel it," he says with excitement.

"I pray that you will."

After about an hour, we part ways and I head back to the house. As I near the shed, with the help of the moonlight, I see a dark form emerge from the doorway. I stop in my tracks. The wind rustles the leaves across the ground and over my feet, making me jump.

"Hello, little lady."

"Thank goodness it's just you, Lewis, I breathe as I recognize the man before me."

"What are you doing out here at this hour?" he slurs.

"I couldn't sleep, so I thought I would come out and check on Shadow."

He stumbles towards me and then, smiling, caresses my cheek. "My, you've grown up nice. Quite perty I might say."

I take a step back, fear overcoming me. "Thank you," I stammer. "I'll be headed back to the house now."

He grabs my arm and pulls me towards the shed. I pull back as hard as I can trying to break free, but he is too strong. He throws me against the wall of the shed and I hit with a thud.

"I've seen you visiting that negro at night. I'm not going to allow him to have all the fun," he spits.

I try to get around him, but he grabs me and pins me against the wall. A scream escapes my lips before his hand clamps down over my mouth. I bite down hard until I can taste his blood in my mouth. He yanks his hand back and lets out a yell, bringing his fist down swiftly across my face. Blood begins to trickle down my face as my head starts to spin. I feel Lewis' body close in against mine and I can smell the liquor on his breath.

"Do you give the negro this much trouble, you filthy whore?" he whispers.

I want to move, but I am so dizzy I can't seem to make out which way is up. The burning sensation of bile rises in my throat. *This is it, I'm about to get taken advantage of and there is nothing I can do about it.* I bring my free hand up in one last desperate attempt to break free, raking his eyes with my fingernails. I feel his hold loosen for an instant, so I try to wiggle free, but it is to no avail. He grips my shoulders harder and slams me into the wall again. I feel like my skull is going to split open. My vision keeps going in and out and my arms and legs feel weak.

"That's better. Gotta beat that spunk out of ya. You always were a firecracker. I like that in a woman."

The door creaks open.

"Help me," I whisper weakly.

There is a lot of commotion that I cannot make sense of. All I know is that the weight of Lewis is off of me. I slide down the wall and hold my knees to my chest until I can see straight. I hear a thud and look up to see Benjamin standing in front of me.

Kneeling down, he takes my face in his hands, "Josephine, are you okay? he asks out of breath. "He didn't, did he?" His eyes wide as he waits for my answer.

"No, Benjamin. Thanks to you."

A sigh of relief escapes from his lips as he pulls me into his body, "Thank you, Jesus."

I bury my head into his chest. "Benjamin, I was so scared. I couldn't move or do anything. I could smell his breath and feel his body pressed against mine. I felt so hopeless. If it wasn't for you, he would have."

"Jo, don't even think about that. You are safe and he will never be able to hurt you again. Let me look at your face."

"How bad is it?" I ask wincing as he gently touches it. "It's very tender."

"You still look beautiful," he says with a smile.

Blushing, I look away. Then, I remember.

"Lewis. What are we going to do about him? Is he dead?"

"Yes, I believe so," Benjamin responds.

We think for a minute before deciding to drag him to the creek along with his almost empty bottle of liquor.

"Everyone will think he just lost his balance, hit his head on the rocks, and drowned," Benjamin says.

The plan sounds good enough to me. Benjamin grabs his arms while I grab his legs and we slowly make our way to the creek. Dark clouds whipping across the normally bright harvest moon make it harder to navigate the wooded terrain. The wind rattles the leaves that are left on the trees causing me to freeze in my tracks every few feet just to be sure no one is following us. I drop Lewis twice before we make it to the creek. He is so heavy and my arms ache from the weight of his legs. I try not to look at him as we make our way down through the woods, not wanting to catch a glimpse of his head lolling around between his shoulders, or his wide, open eyes that are staring, but seeing nothing. We finally arrive at the creek bank and sling his limp body into the water along with his bottle of liquor.

Benjamin takes my face in his hands and looks me in the

eyes. "Are you sure you are okay?"

"Yes, I am okay. I can't thank you enough," I say as I take his hands in mine.

He kisses me on the forehead and we walk back to the house.

"We speak to no one of this, no matter what happens. Agree?" Benjamin whispers.

"Yes. As far as I am concerned, this nightmare never happened," I reply quietly before we go our separate ways.

I close the door to my room and wince. I can feel every bone in my body aching, especially my head. I climb into bed and lay there trying to process the events of the last few hours. How scared I was when Lewis attacked me. What will happen if no one believes Lewis actually drowned? How am I going to explain the bruising on my face? What is this feeling I keep getting around Benjamin every time he looks at me or touches me? I can still feel the warmth of his kiss on my forehead. I smile thinking of him as I close my eyes to try to find sleep.

A restless sleep came and before I know it Millie is in my room. She looks at me.

"What happened to you? Did you fall coming back from one of your visits with Benjamin?"

My mouth drops.

"Did you think I didn't know? I see you sneaking around with him. You are not the only one, you know. He has a way with all of us women. For some reason, we can't seem to resist that smile of his and the way he looks at us. How do you think I got into this predicament?" As she says this, she rubs her hand across her stomach. My eyes widen. I had noticed that Millie was looking a little thicker around the middle, but I never thought that was the reason why.

I feel ill. "You...you're with child?" I barely whisper.

"Yes, but don't say anything to Benjamin. He doesn't know yet. I want to surprise him."

Now that I think about it, Benjamin has been walking Millie to the slave quarters in the evening an awful lot. I am quite confused. He rarely talks about Millie, and even when he does, he never has much good to say about her, just that she is always moody, depressed, and just a regular ole stick in the mud. Maybe this is his way of keeping me from seeing the way he truly feels about her. But then why does he look at me the way he does and touch me so gently? My blood begins to boil. Does he care for me at all or am I just a pawn in his game? Just another woman he has fooled, because apparently, he has many according to Millie. If nothing else, I thought he was my friend. Why would he treat me this way?

"Would you like me to help you get dressed?" Millie asks, bringing me out of my thoughts.

"No, Millie, I don't feel well. Please tell everyone I won't be down today."

"Did I say something to upset you?" Millie asks slyly.

"Leave, Millie."

She throws me a smug smile as she leaves the room.

I lay back down, head throbbing and body still aching from last night. I can't believe this. After all we have been through, it is all just a game to him? I can't believe this. I won't believe it. But Millie is definitely pregnant. I can't think about this any longer. It's making my head hurt even worse. I close my eyes and when I open them again, the sun is high in the sky. Feeling better after more rest, I get out of bed and make my way downstairs. Everyone is downstairs around the table getting ready to partake in a rather extravagant meal. There is food everywhere. I am rather confused for a minute, but then

I see him.

"John, you made it home!" I exclaim.

Everyone turns.

"Jo, what happened to your face?" Mother asks in horror.

John runs over to me.

"It's rather embarrassing. I fell down the stairs last night," I say in between John poking around at my face.

"There doesn't appear to be anything broken. Just a lot of swelling and bruising. It should heal in a week or so," he says. "That must have been quite a tumble."

"Yes, all the way down. My whole body is rather sore, but my hard head took the brunt of it," I reply laughing.

"I'm glad you're okay Jo. If you're feeling up to it, we are just about to eat. Have a seat," Father says happily.

I sit and we eat a delicious meal. It feels so good to be back together as a family again. I have missed John a great deal in the past few years.

John has changed so much. He is taller and speaks with an air of confidence he has never had before. I am thinking about this when I hear a question that makes my heart leap into my throat.

"John, did you happen to see Lewis in town when you came through?"

"No, Father, I did not. Did he not show up for work today?"

"No, he did not, which is very much unlike him. Although he has other vices, not showing up for work is not one of them. Will you ride around with me and help me look for him?"

"Yes, sir."

It isn't long before Father and John come back with Lewis slumped over my father's horse, Bandit.

My mother runs out and I follow, but more slowly.

"Oh no, what happened?" Mother asks in shock.

"It looks like he had a bit too much to drink and slipped and fell into the creek. Hit his head on a rock and drowned," I hear my father telling my mother as I walk towards them. Father had a hold of the liquor bottle. I breathe a sigh of relief and say a quick prayer of thanks that our plan worked.

Frannie, Ann, Delilah, Benjamin, and Millie came out to see what was going on. John tells them what happened. Frannie, Ann, and Delilah bow their heads in silent prayer, but Millie turns to Benjamin and wraps her arms around his neck and kisses him on the cheek. He returns her hug and whispers something in her ear. Millie turns and smiles at me. I turn my back on them and walk back into the house. That is all the confirmation I need.

The next few weeks I avoid Benjamin like the plague. Ann and Delilah keep asking me what happened between us, but I can't find the words to tell them. Benjamin is out with my father one November afternoon, or so I think, so I head to the stable to visit Shadow. As she nibbles a treat from my hand, I hear someone come in to the stable.

"Why won't you talk to me anymore?" Benjamin demands.

I shake my head, "I can't Benjamin, because if I do, I will get caught up in your game."

"What are you talking about?"

"I know about Millie and the other girls you have in your life and I will not be one of them. If you ask me, you should grow up and take responsibility for what you have created."

"I still have no idea what you are talking about. What have I created?"

"I guess Millie hasn't told you yet. It's not my place to tell, so maybe you should go ask Millie and stop annoying me!" I scream as I march out of the stable.

Chapter 25

The next day I wake up to a cold drizzle. *Great, a day that reflects my mood.* I roll over to get out of bed, become tangled up in the covers, and fall onto the floor. Grabbing my pillow, I hit it against the bed a few times. This seems to be my attitude lately. I am just angry at everything. I can't believe I cared so much for someone who was just making a fool of me. *You were just friends, Josephine. It was only a friendship, nothing more.* A friendship that we both knew would eventually end because we were from two different worlds. I should have listened to my mother years ago and realized this sooner. It would have saved me the heartache now.

"Have you told Benjamin?" I ask Millie as she comes in to help me get dressed.

"He come up to me yesterday and ask me why you said what you said."

"So, you told him?"

"Yes, I told him and he so happy. He says we gonna jump the broom tonight and I be his forever."

I can't speak. I leave the room, headed for the stable. I can always think better there. I am just hoping I don't run into Benjamin. I step outside and wrap my arms around me to shield myself from the cold rain.

"Josephine!" I turn and Delilah is frantically waving me into the smokehouse.

"Is everything okay?" I ask worriedly as I step inside. Warmth and the smell of delicious food hits me as I enter.

"Everything is absolutely wonderful. Sit down, child."

I'm glad someone is happy. I think as I sit down in the nearest chair.

"Benjamin wanted to tell you, but he is away with your father. Some poor slaves are getting sold today, God be with them. He asked me to tell you because it is very important and he insisted it cannot wait until he gets back."

I feel bile form in my throat.

"Save your breath," I snap. "I know what he wants to tell me. Millie already told me. They are jumping the broom tonight. I have to go now."

"Sit back down, child, and listen to me," Delilah commands.

I am shocked. I don't know what else to do other than obey, so I sit back down.

"You know there is more between you two than the law allows."

"It's just a friendship, Delilah, or was a friendship."

"Whatever you say, Josephine. Anyway, whatever happened between you and Benjamin yesterday in the barn caused Benjamin to confront Millie. Thank the good Lord he did, because I couldn't bear to see you two going on the way you have been the past few weeks. He has been an absolute pain to be around. She finally came clean and told him what she had said to you to cause all of this grief. Child, Benjamin is not the father of Millie's baby. Lewis is the father. Only reason Benjamin was walking Millie to her quarters was because Lewis had been taking advantage of Millie and even though

191

Benjamin isn't fond of her, he still didn't want that happening to her. You know you are the only woman that Benjamin cares for. God help you both."

I can't believe it. My happiness quickly turns to anger though when I think of Millie. She has caused me nothing but trouble my whole life and almost destroyed my most important friendship.

"Thank you so much," I say kissing Delilah on the cheek. "I am so glad you have put my mind at ease about Benjamin. Now, I must go find Millie."

I walk in the house, slamming the door as I go.

"Young lady, we do not slam doors here," Mother chastises as she comes out of the study.

"I'm sorry, Mother, I am very angry right now."

"Don't be angry, dear, he's just a useless slave anyway. I wish you would get that through your head."

"What are you talking about?" I ask stopping mid-step.

"That's why you are mad, isn't it? Your father is selling that coachman of ours. What's his name, Benjamin or something like that?"

My heart skips several beats.

"What? Why is he selling Benjamin? Which town are they going too?" I ask frantically.

"It's that big sale they are having in Washington. Wait, where are you going?"

I don't answer. I am already half way up the stairs running to my room. This cannot happen. I have to stop this. I grab my cape before finding Millie cleaning my mother's room. I grab her by the arm and drag her down the stairs and outside. The cold rain starts beating harder as we near the stable.

"Tom, saddle up Shadow!" I shout.

"Yes, ma'am. I get her right quick for ya, little missy."

I push Millie up onto Shadow and settle in behind her. Digging my heels into Shadow, we take off at breakneck speed towards Washington. The cold rain soaks us in minutes and stings our faces as we barrel down the road.

"Slow down, Josephine, we going too fast and I's scared!"

"Shut up, Millie. I don't want to hear anything you have to say. I have tried to be nice to you my whole life considering your circumstance. I even planned on setting you and your baby free as soon as it was born. You have been nothing but mean and hateful back to me. I am done with you, Millie."

"What are you gonna do?"

"My father is selling Benjamin. I am going to buy him back."

"Why are you bringing me?"

"I need money to buy him, Millie."

She turns to look at me and I see fear in her eyes. I avert my attention back to the road that is quickly turning to mud.

"You gonna sell me!"

"I am going to do whatever it takes to get Benjamin back, and if that means selling you, so be it."

Millie starts flailing and trying to jump off Shadow.

"You say you'd never sell me. Say you never gonna be like your family, say you gonna set me free!"

"Plans have changed, Millie. You have brought this upon yourself, telling me you and Benjamin were going to jump the broom tonight and you were having his baby. I've tried to be nice to you and let things go considering your circumstance, but you have crossed me one too many times. Now stop flailing!"

"I won't let you sell me, I won't. I kill you first!"

"That's enough!" I scream as I bring my fist down across the

193

side of her head. She immediately falls limp and I struggle to balance her to keep her from falling off Shadow. I look upon her appalled. *What have I done? What am I doing? This isn't me. This is not who I am.* I quickly feel for a pulse to make sure I haven't killed her. Thankfully it is still beating. I come to a fork in the road and instead of steering Shadow right towards Washington, I guide her left. *Lord, please don't let me be too late to buy Benjamin.* It isn't long before I come to a tiny farm house at the end of the road. *I hope this is the place my aunt has been speaking of.* I ride around to the back of the house.

"Millie, wake up," I say shaking her gently. "This is your stop."

She groans and looks around groggily, "Please don't sell me Missy Josephine. Please," she says as she places her hand to her head.

"Millie, I'm not going to sell you. That's not who I am. I'm sorry. I don't know what came over me. You lying to me and the thought of losing Benjamin pushed me over the edge. Please, Millie, we must hurry and get inside," I say as I help steady her as she dismounts.

"Where are we?"

"They are friends, Millie. They will take good care of you."

She turns and looks at me wide-eyed, "You said you weren't going to sell me. You lied!"

"Hush, Millie. I'm not selling you. I'm setting you free. I want you and your baby to be free," I say as I knock on the door.

"Who is it?" A voice comes from inside.

"A friend," I respond.

A round faced woman opens the door and ushers me and Millie inside quickly. She eyes me suspiciously, "What can I help you with?"

I take a deep breath, "I have come here, because my Aunt Diane has told me about this place. I need some help, please."

"You're Josephine?"

"Yes ma'am," I say as I breathe a sigh of relief.

"Your aunt has told me a lot about you and she said you may be on my doorstep one day. This one going somewhere?" she asks smiling.

"Yes, and she is going as a free woman. May I borrow a piece of parchment and a quill?"

The woman shuffles through a nearby desk and then hands the items to me. I write the free paper for Millie as quickly as I can and hand it to her.

"Good luck, Millie. I hope you stay safe on your journey and you and your baby live a happy and peaceful life," I say as I turn to leave.

"Missy Josephine?"

"Yes, Millie."

"Thank you. I's sorry for all da trouble I cause you and I hope you find Benjamin. He love you, you know. You all he ever want and I always hated you for that, but you good Missy Josephine and I can't thank you enough for what you doin'."

"If I were you, Millie, I would have acted the same way, probably worse. You just take care of yourself and that baby, okay?"

"Yes ma'am, I will. I'll take care of myself and baby Josephine," she says as she cradles her belly.

Emotions overwhelm me. I grab Millie and hug her tightly before I turn and leave. I step out into the cold rain, mount Shadow quickly, and head towards Washington. What I am going to do for money to buy Benjamin back, I don't know. All

I can think of to do is pray and I pray hard the whole way. It seems like an eternity, but Shadow and I finally make it. I am soaked to the bone, but I hardly feel it. I am too numb from the thought of losing Benjamin. I quickly dismount and run to the edge of the crowd.

"Benjamin! Benjamin!" I scream loudly. My lungs feel like they are on fire.

Some of the people in the crowd turn to look at me. A gentleman, one of my father's friends, walks up to me. "Who are you looking for?"

"Benjamin, my father's driver," I gasp between breaths.

"You're too late, he's already gone."

"No!" I scream. "Where is my father?" I demand.

"Sorry, ma'am. The last time I saw your father, he was headed to Thomas Marshall's house. Is everything okay, Josephine?"

I don't respond. I quickly mount Shadow and head to Thomas Marshall's house. Furious, I need to know why my father has sold Benjamin and to whom. The Marshall house is easy to find, being a large brick house set on beautiful acres of land. I have been here many times for various parties, but now I am on a mission. I ride around to the stable to get Shadow out of the wet and cold weather. I can tell she is worn out. I don't think she has ever been ridden this hard. I enter the stable.

"Jo, what are you doing here?"

"Benjamin," I gasp. I drop the reins and without thinking run into his arms and kiss him with everything I have. "I thought, I thought I'd lost you," I say as I cling to him.

"What do you mean? Jo, you're soaked. You must be freezing."

"I'll be fine. Mother told me you were being sold. My father isn't selling you, is he?"

"Not that I know of. Everyone we brought here has already been sold and he told me we were going to spend the night here and go back home tomorrow."

"Oh, thank God," I say as I bury my head into his chest. "Benjamin, I must tell you something that I am ashamed of and I hope you don't think differently of me after I tell you.

"What is it, Jo? You know you can tell me anything," he says as he pulls me back to search my eyes.

I look away, ashamed about what I am going to tell him.

"I had just found out that Millie lied to me about her baby being yours. I was furious and then when I walked into the house, Mother told me you were being sold. I snapped. I found Millie and dragged her out with the intention of selling her in order to get the money to buy you. On the way here, I hit her so hard that I knocked her out. I swore I would never buy or sell someone, but the thought of losing you was more than I could fathom and I was bound and determined to get you back no matter the consequences."

"You didn't sell her, did you?" he asked with fear and pain in his eyes.

"No, I couldn't go through with it. I came to my senses and I took her to a safe house and set her free. They will see she gets safely north."

"Then why would I be ashamed of you?"

"Because I lost control and had the thought to sell her. I fear I am no different than my family."

"Josephine," Benjamin said while taking my face in his hands and looking into my eyes. "You are nothing like your family. You lost your temper and you were angry and scared. We all have thoughts at times that we shouldn't. The fact that you

197

didn't act on them and you set Millie free. Josephine, you did the right thing and that makes me love you even more," he says as he pulls me in and holds me tightly.

A sigh of relief escapes my lips as I melt into his embrace.

"I was so scared I was going to lose you today."

"Josephine, if we ever do get separated, just remember that I will never forget you. You will always be in my heart. Always remember that. I love you Jo. I always have."

"I love you Benjamin. I always will."

He kisses me once more before I make my way around to the main entrance. I knock on the door only then realizing how wet and cold I am. I start to shiver uncontrollably. Finally, the door opens and I step into the foyer.

"Josephine, what are you doing here? You are completely drenched."

"Millie had crossed me one time too many, Father, and I wanted to get her down here as quickly as I could and sell her before the auction was over," I lied.

"Tillie, draw up a hot bath for Miss Josephine," Thomas orders a nearby slave.

"Thank you, Mr. Marshall. I'm sorry for dripping water all over your rug."

"No need to worry, young lady. Your health is more important. Go dry off before you get sick."

"Thank you, sir."

I follow Tillie as she leads me to the bath. I happily sink into the warm water and let it relax my tense muscles. I ask for God's forgiveness for withholding the truth from my father as I lay down in one of the Marshall's spare bedrooms. I fall asleep thinking of Benjamin and how wonderful it felt to be in his arms and feel his lips on mine.

Chapter 26

Days go by and thankfully no one questions Lewis' death or where the money is that I would have received for selling Millie. John finally opens his practice in Augusta and against my mother's wishes, I travel there a couple times a week and assist him with patients and tidy up his facility. John tried to help smooth things over with my mother by explaining to her that Florence Nightingale, an upper-class British woman, took part in nursing duties during the Crimean War, and that many lives were saved due to her work. My mother did not want to hear it though. She said there is a reason we separated from Britain. As soon as I mentioned that I could possibly find a beau by being in town though, she finally relented and accepts it.

I learn so much from John. He holds so much knowledge about the human body and is eager to share it with me. I learn how to properly bandage a wound and what to do to break a fever. I even enjoy the rides to town and back home. They allow plenty of time for me to think about Benjamin and how our lives could move forward together. We have come up with many ideas on how to solve our problem but none of them, we realize, will work. We would always be living in fear. One of my ideas was to forge free papers for him so we could leave one night, but understandably Benjamin did not want to leave his mother and grandmother behind in the bonds of slavery. When I told Ann and Delilah that they could come with us, Delilah would not have it. She said she was too old to be running away and she would only slow us down. Then there was the fear of us getting caught. I'm not sure what would happen to me, but Benjamin, Ann, and Delilah would be hung for sure. I couldn't allow that to happen. As of right now, we are all safe, healthy, and together - that is all that matters to us at the moment, especially since there is so much tension building between the northern and southern states. There is not a day that goes by that my father does not have some news on the rift in the democratic party and how that rift will surely lead to the election of the republican party's nominee, Abraham Lincoln. If that happens, he says, the southern states will secede from the union and he hopes Kentucky will be one of them. He says that our lives as we know them depend on slavery, and without it, we will lose everything.

I listen closely to everything my father says and even eavesdrop when other prominent men of the area come to visit my father, because they always discuss the current events. I absorb everything like a sponge and then discuss it all with Benjamin in the evenings. I don't know what I want. I want Mr. Lincoln to be elected president, because I want an end to slavery, but I am concerned about Kentucky and the other states seceding from the union. Will the union allow that? Will this start a war? What will happen to my family? These thoughts haunt my rides to town.

It is a chilly, rainy day in April, so I pull my cape tighter around my body as Shadow and I make our trip to Augusta. I am thinking about how much has changed since Abraham

Lincoln has been elected president. Several states have seceded from the union and there is so much tension between the states that I am afraid that war is inevitable. As we work our way through the bustling streets, I can tell there is excitement in the air. I dismount and hurry inside to see if John knows what is going on. He meets me at the door.

"Did you hear?"

"No, what is going on? Everybody seems different today."

"The Confederates fired on Fort Sumter and now Lincoln has asked for volunteer soldiers to take up arms against them. We are at war."

"You aren't going to go off and fight, are you?" I ask worriedly.

"No, I would never fight for the union and this war is going to be over before I could even make it to enlist anyway. I hate to say it, but the North is going to win this war easily. They have so many more people and provisions available than we do. I'm just going to stay here and continue to take care of the people in this town."

I breathe a sigh of relief. I do not want my brother to risk his life fighting to keep others in bondage. I secretly pray the North will win and do it quickly.

The next couple months go by without too much noticeable change. I continue to act as nurse for John and life on the farm carries on as usual. My father travels to Natchez to sell more slaves and Benjamin and I sneak in as much time together as we can, discussing the war and planning what we would do if the North won and he was freed.

It's a hot July day and I descend the stairs to find my Aunt Diane and John talking to my mother in the parlor. Mother has tears in her eyes, which alarms me, because she never cries.

"Your brother has decided to assist in the war," Mother says when she sees me entering the room.

"What do you mean by assist? John, you told me you weren't going to fight and that the North would win the war quickly."

"Diane brought me news that the first land battle has been fought and the Confederates held their ground and pushed the Northern troops back to D.C. with their tails between their legs," he relates to me. "It looks like the South has a chance and that this war may last longer than both sides expected. But before you get all upset with me as Mother has, I am going as a surgeon, not as a soldier. I will leave for Virginia tomorrow. When Diane told me of all the men that were wounded, I knew what God was asking of me. I cannot just sit back as men suffer. I am needed on the front."

"John, I know better than to argue with you, because I can tell you have already made up your mind. All I will say is that I am going to miss you terribly and please be safe," I say as I hug him tightly.

"Diane," Mother says turning to my aunt. "I know we have always had different views on certain ways of life, but I wish you safe travels."

"Safe travels? Diane, where are you going?" I ask concerned.

"Your brother is not the only one who is being called to aid in the war. I am going to travel to D.C. and see if I can be of assistance in any way."

"And what am I supposed to do, sit back while everybody leaves? John, let me go with you, I am a good nurse."

"You will do nothing of the sort! Helping John in Augusta is one thing, but traipsing all over chasing battles and being around all those soldiers is another. I will not allow it. Besides, I need you around here, especially now that your father is in

Natchez."

"She's right Jo, it will not be safe for you," John agrees.

"Diane is going. It won't be safe for her either."

"I am used to being on my own. I will be fine, but a beautiful, young woman like yourself. No, Jo, it wouldn't be safe. I have to agree with your mother on this one."

"Then if I can't go, I want you both to write as often as you can. I want to make sure you both are safe. Please be safe." I hug them both and watch through teary eyes as they depart. I can't help but wonder what it must be like to have two men leaving from the same family, yet fighting for different sides. At least John and Diane, although joining different sides, will never be aiming muskets at each other. As I make my way to the stable, I pray that God will be with them both and keep them safe.

Chapter 27

"This place just isn't the same without your brother and Diane being around, is it?" Mother asks sadly.

"No, the last few months haven't been normal at all. Thank goodness their letters are making it through to us," I respond as I open a new letter from Diane.

Dear Josephine,

I hope this letter finds you well. I am writing to let you know that I am safe and healthy. I have found my place working long hours as a nurse in a D.C. hospital, caring for all the wounded men. The situation here is very sad. The soldiers are not only hospitalized due to wounds, but illness is quickly sweeping through the regiments as well. I pray the war ends soon. I am already tired of seeing men wounded, sick, and dying.

Yours Truly,

Diane

Diane's letter is disturbing, which makes the job I am getting ready for on this September day all the more important. I am getting ready to attend a lady's aid meeting in Augusta. Mother and I don't sit idly and wait for the war to end, we do our part attending various tea parties held by the ladies' aid societies, where we roll bandages and gather other supplies needed for the wounded men. I attend those for the Confederate troops as well as the Union troops. Although I want the North to win the war, I have family and friends fighting for the Confederates and I will be unable to live with myself if I ignore their needs as well. Mother despises that I attend those held for the Union troops, but I have smoothed it over with her by telling her that I am gathering supplies that Diane may need. She has kept her mouth shut since then, but I can tell she disapproves every time I leave for one. This is a day that I will be attending a meeting by myself. The glares from my mother are piercing as I head for the door, but before I can make it out, Benjamin walks in with a letter.

"Sorry ma'am, this letter was overlooked in the saddlebag."

"That's ok, Benjamin, thank you very much. Mother, it's a letter from John!" I exclaim.

I open it quickly and read it aloud so my mother and father can hear.

"It's dated April 8th, 1862."

Dear Mother, Father, and Josephine,

I hope this letter reaches you and finds you all well. I am in Shiloh, Tennessee where a two-day battle has just ended. The casualties have been numerous and it saddens me to say that our very own General Albert Sidney Johnston is among them. The wounded keep pouring in and I continue to find myself overwhelmed every day by numerous amputations and soldiers with entrails hanging from their abdomens. These men are brought to my tent mangled and in agony. I have removed so many limbs, many without any type of anesthesia. The screams of the men haunt me when I close my eyes and I often have nightmares that I am drowning in their blood. I am exhausted and I pray that this war ends soon. I am sorry to bring you such depressing news, but this is the reality of war. I must get back to work now, the men need me.

All my love,

John

I fold the letter up, hand it to Father, turn and leave. I cannot speak for fear of shedding tears. The picture my brother has portrayed is horrible and it is consuming my thoughts as I ride Shadow to Augusta. How terrifying it must be to engage in battle, to kill another and potentially face death yourself. I am eventually pulled out of my thoughts by a noise to my left. I turn to see Confederate soldiers standing on the hill looking down over Augusta. *What are they doing here?* I dig my heels into Shadow to make her pick up speed and quickly arrive at Front Street where the meeting is being held. I knock on the door.

"Come in, quickly. It looks like the Home Guard is preparing for battle," says Edna, the head of the ladies aid.

"I saw Confederates on the hill. I was hoping they were just passing through. Surely there is not going to be a battle here."

At that moment a loud boom rattles the windows. I run to the window and peek out. "The gunboat, Belfast, has just fired a shell!" I exclaim.

"Come away from the window, Josephine, it is not safe," one of the women implores me.

Boom. Boom. Two more shells are fired from the Belfast. The sound is deafening.

"Surely the Confederates won't attack, not against a warship," Sally says hopefully.

We watch as a shell barely misses the Belfast. Then we hear the Rebel yell.

I turn to face the other ladies in the group, "We must arm ourselves."

"You don't think they would harm us, do you?" Edna asks.

"I'm not sure, but I don't want to take any chances."

The seven of us arm ourselves with all of the knives we can find. Huddling under the staircase, we listen wide-eyed at the commotion around us. Edna begins praying and others join in. I sit quietly in silent prayer, listening to the sounds. I can hear men and women shouting, muskets firing, and shells whizzing through the air. Then it happened in an instant: a shell came through the back of the house. The blast knocks me against the wall. I feel disoriented as a ringing begins in my ears. Smoke and debris fill the room. I can see others in my group trying to get their bearings as well, but no one appears to be seriously injured.

"Everyone out! The house is on fire!" Edna screams.

I head for the door amidst the frenzy and fling it open only to come face to face with a Confederate.

"Frederick!" I exclaim astonished. I try to slam the door, but he moves too quickly. He puts his hand out and catches it, forcing it in.

"Scatter out, men. This one here is mine," he says with a smirk on his face as he walks towards me.

I back up against the wall, concealing the knife behind my skirt.

"Fancy running into you under these circumstances," Frederick says as he places the barrel of the revolver against my temple.

"Please, Frederick, don't hurt me," I plead.

"I always knew you were behind our slaves running away. You may have been able to fool everyone else, but not me. I knew you were trouble the first time I laid eyes on you. You won't be trouble anymore though. I'm going to enjoy watching your blood splatter all over this wall."

"You know what?" I ask barely above a whisper.

"What?" He asks leaning in closer to me.

I thrust the knife into his abdomen, turn it, and pull up.

"I'm going to enjoy watching your insides spill out onto the floor."

He falls with a thud, his entrails sprawling out around him. I grab his revolver and peer around the room. The smoke is so thick that I can barely see. A couple of the ladies that I have spent many an hour with lay dead on the floor, bullet wounds right between their eyes. They stare blankly at the ceiling.

"Please don't shoot me, please!" Edna howls.

I aim and fire hitting the Confederate in the back. He collapses onto Edna. She screams and pushes him off of her in disgust. I grab her hand and we run outside. Coughing, teary eyed, and glad to be out in the fresh air, I breathe deeply to expel the smoke from my lungs. The streets are in complete chaos. People are running, screaming, and engaging in hand to hand combat. Women and children wave white handkerchiefs in surrender from windows as men shoot from those same windows. Houses and stores are on fire, filling the air with thick, black smoke. I look out across the river and notice that the gunboats have left. *Why would they leave us when we need them?* I can't worry about that right now, though, because Edna and I need to get to safety. We sneak around to the side of the house and hide behind the bushes until the fighting ceases. When no more shots are heard for a while, Edna and I creep out of our hiding place to find that the militia has surrendered. The Confederates are looting the stores and rounding up prisoners.

"What do we do now?" Edna asks over the groans of the injured.

I look around.

"We tend to the wounded."

I begin ripping up my petticoats as Edna watches me with astonishment.

"What are you doing?"

"We need bandages. You should do the same, and quickly."

I hurry to the nearest downed civilian. He lay face down on the ground, writhing in pain. I roll him over slowly and immediately turn to the side and wretch. I have never seen such a sight. Half of his arm is missing, blown off by a shell. There is jagged bone and muscle exposed and blood soaking his shirt. I start to panic, not knowing what to do. The man's cries fill my ears. I close my eyes and take a couple of steadying breaths. *Relax, these people need you. You can do this.* I open my eyes and look at the man's face. I have seen him around before on my many trips into town.

"You are going to be okay," I assure with a smile. Then I begin to work. I tie a bandage around his arm to stop the bleeding. I can feel the jagged bone under my fingers as I work so I quickly try to think of something else. As I'm finishing up, a boy appears in tears.

"Father!" he yells as he wraps his arms around his dad's neck.

"It's okay son, I am okay. This woman has helped me. Thank you so much, ma'am," he says through gritted teeth, trying to hide his pain from his son.

"They are making a hospital out of a house down the street. I will take you there," the young boy says.

I help the gentleman up and wish him the best. As they walk away, I see Edna waving to me from a nearby house. "Josephine, I need your help!"

I run into the house after her and almost slip and fall.

209

The room is covered in blood and the smell is horrendous. Bodies are on top of bodies on the staircase. Gray coats are intertwined with blue coats, and mixed in are the varied clothing of civilians. Edna vomits before rushing out of the house.

I go to the nearest person. He is a Confederate, but I don't care, all I see is a person in need. He reaches for me and I grab his hand. There is a large wound in his abdomen and his breathing is labored.

"Are you an angel?" he asks.

"No, sir, I am just here to help."

"I don't think there is any help for me," he says as he starts to weep, causing him to cough violently. Blood splatters from his mouth.

I don't know what to do. I don't want to give him any false hope, so I just squeeze his hand tighter and wipe the sweat from his brow. It isn't long before his breathing becomes more and more shallow and his hand releases from mine. I fold his hands together on his abdomen, and fighting back tears, place the cloth over his wide-open eyes. I get up quickly and move to the next wounded person. I work tirelessly into the night, transporting the wounded, patching them up, and comforting the dying. I escort my final patient to the hospital and ask if my services are needed there. The nurse thanks me, but says that I have done enough and to get some rest. As I walk away from the hospital, I can hear a man pleading with the doctor not to take his leg. I shudder at the thought. I am exhausted, both physically and mentally. *I need to get home.* Then I remember Shadow.

"Shadow!" I scream as I run towards the remains of Edna's house. My thoughts are everywhere. What if she is injured, dead, or taken by the soldiers? How could I have let her down? I am so mad at myself. I run as fast as I can, but stop short when I see someone on horseback coming right at me. I duck behind a tree. After enough close calls today, I am not going to take my chance with a stranger on horseback. I attempt to slow my breathing down. The beating of the hooves gets closer. By this time, it sounds like there are two horses. *Great, now there are two men.* I slide quietly down the tree to make myself as small as possible. The horses stop by the tree and I hold my breath. *Should I make a run for it?* One of the riders dismounts and I take off running as fast as my legs can carry me, but I don't make it very far before I am grabbed from behind and lifted into the air. I start desperately kicking and screaming.

"Josephine, it's me, it's okay, it's okay. It's Benjamin."

I stop flailing as he puts me down. I turn and fall into his arms. I spill out all the events of the day. From Edna's house being shelled, to the fire and Frederick, the countless men, women, and children that I tended to, and Shadow.

He listens and comforts me until I am finished, then takes my face in his hands and kisses me.

"I'm glad you are okay. That must have been terrifying. I wish I could have been here with you to protect you and fight alongside the Home Guard."

"I'm glad you weren't here," I say shaking my head. "They took many able men as prisoners. I couldn't imagine what they would do to you if you were taken prisoner." I shudder at the thought.

He pulls me in and holds me tightly.

"Come here, I have someone I want you to see." He leads me around the tree where I see Shadow nibbling on a bush.

"Shadow!" I hug her neck tightly, feeling her warmth and

211

taking in her scent.

"I knew something was wrong when she came home without you. Your mother sent me straight out to look for you. I was scared to death when I smelled the smoke as I neared the city and then saw the damage to some of the buildings."

"How did you find me?"

"I heard you scream for Shadow. Quite the set of lungs you have," he says smiling as he helps me into the saddle.

I must have fallen asleep during the ride home, because the next thing I comprehend is Ann gasping, "What happened?"

I look around to find that we are in the stable. Benjamin helps me down as he describes to Ann about the attack on Augusta.

Delilah and Ann usher me into the house after learning of the events and begin preparing my bath and helping me out of my dress. Mother comes in and looks in horror at my blood-stained dress, face, and hands. I tell her that Morgan's Raiders, led by Colonel Basil Duke, led an attack on Augusta. The Home Guard, along with many civilians, countered that attack. I tell her everything, except the fact that I killed Frederick and another Confederate. She would probably disown me if I told her that, even though they were going to kill me.

"Who won?" she asks.

"The Confederates."

"Praise the Almighty."

She leaves me to clean up. The warm water feels so incredible as I ease my sore body into it. I scrub the blood off of me and pray for the wounded and the deceased as I do. I stay in the water just long enough to get clean, because the bloody water makes me nauseous and reminds me of the floors in the houses. I slide into my nightgown and head for my room.

Father catches me before I can get there to make sure I am okay and asks me if I want any breakfast. The thought of food makes me ill, so I politely decline and continue to my room. The sun is coming up as I lay my head on my pillow. I pray that sleep overcomes me quickly so I don't have to continue to see the faces of the wounded when I close my eyes. Thankfully, it does.

Chapter 28

"I can't believe we are celebrating another Christmas without John and Diane at home," I say sadly.

"Hopefully this will be the last," Father responds.

"But only if the South wins. I hope this war goes on forever unless the South wins," Mother interjects.

"How can you say something like that, Mother? There are men dying every day on both sides in battle, fathers and brothers. Our very own John and Diane are in and out of danger caring for these wounded and sick men. Diane's most recent letter speaks of her attending to men on the battlefield while bullets and artillery are being fired all around her. John is amputating limbs and digging shrapnel out of men as cannon balls are exploding dangerously close to his makeshift surgical room, which is usually no more than a tent! So please, Mother, tell me how you can say that?"

"Clearly, I am the only one here who is devoted to the southern cause."

"The Southern cause, Mother, is to remain apart from the rest of the country in order to continue to enslave human beings."

"And what is wrong with that, young lady? Has the business of slavery not put clothes on your back and food on our table?"

"Prostitution can do that as well. Do you think that is an acceptable way of living, Mother?"

Whack! I reach up where my mother has just slapped me, my skin still tingling from the blow.

"I will not have you speak to me in that way again, young lady."

"Why, because you know I am right?"

"Josephine!" my father's voice booms. "Leave this room now. I will not allow such disrespect."

I leave without another word. *No wonder we are at war,* I think. *My family can't even have a civilized conversation about slavery, how is a whole country supposed to discuss it and come to a reasonable conclusion?*

Chapter 29

"Happy New Year, Mary," I greet as I walk into our parlor. "What brings you here today? Have you heard from Oliver lately?"

"I received a letter a few days ago. He had just fought in the second battle at Manassas. He said he and his fellow Confederates were outnumbered by the Union army, but they fought hard and defeated the Union troops. He said they were getting ready to push further north to take the Northern capital. That was about four months ago, Jo! I wish the mail could get to us sooner. I search the casualty list after every battle. I don't know how much more of this I can take. What if he has been taken prisoner, is wounded, or worse, dead? I wish this war was over, I hate it!"

"I do as well, Mary. Oliver is a strong and smart man and he will do whatever it takes to make it back to you safely. All we can do is pray that he stays safe and that the war ends quickly. Delilah, will you please get Mary a cup of tea? It will help calm your nerves, Mary."

"Thank you, Jo, but it will take more than tea to calm my nerves. Father went into town today and he said that Lincoln has issued a revision to his Emancipation Proclamation that he issued after the Union victory at Sharpsburg. All of the border states are still excluded from freeing our slaves, thank goodness, but he is allowing negroes into the Union army! Father said we are going to have to start shackling our slaves at night. We can't have them running off and fighting against our boys. I'm afraid, Jo. What if this gives our slaves ideas and courage to slaughter us in our beds at night? I'm going to make sure the overseer double checks those shackles every night."

"I am afraid too," I respond absentmindedly. *But not for the same reasons,* I thought. My thoughts are on Benjamin. I know he is going to want to be the first in line to fight for his freedom and that scares me more than anything.

Chapter 30

"Is it true, Jo?" Benjamin asks anxiously as soon as I walk into the stable.

"Is what true?" I ask reluctantly, already knowing what he is referring to.

"Is Lincoln calling for colored folk to take up arms and fight for the Union?"

"Yes, but I forbid you to leave."

"What? You can't do that. Didn't he also free all slaves as well? I am a free man."

"He freed all slaves within the rebel states. Kentucky did not secede from the Union; therefore, you are still my father's property and I forbid you to join the Union troops."

"Since when did you start accepting and enforcing slavery?" Benjamin demands angrily.

"Since I learned that someone I care for dearly is allowed to become a soldier. Benjamin, you can't go off to war. I have seen men with limbs hanging from their bodies, half blown off. I have heard their screams of pain and agony and watched as men died because their entrails were hanging from their abdomens. I've watched blood squirt out from severed arteries with each and every heartbeat, strong and vigorous at first and then slower and slower until their heart stops pumping and the life leaves their body. How am I supposed to sleep at night, knowing that one day one of those scenarios could be you?"

"Jo, I cannot stay here knowing that freedom is so close. If the Union wins this war, my family will be free and we will be able to have a life together. You have done so much to protect me and my family. This is my chance to be a man, not a slave."

I can see the fire and passion in his eyes as he speaks. *He is going to go whether I allow him to or not.* I shake my head while grabbing his hands and hold them tightly, "Okay, but please, please stay safe and come back to me when the war is over."

"I will do my best to come back to you," he says as he leans in and kisses me quickly.

"Now all we need is a plan to get you enlisted."

Word quickly spreads that Maysville is enlisting colored men into the Federal troops, so I decide to pay a visit to my grandmother in Maysville. Mother and Father agree that it would be a good idea to visit her and to get away from the country for a while. I watch as Benjamin hugs his mother and grandmother and then he helps me into the carriage. I make sure to bring extra blankets since the February air is quite cold and I hunker down amongst them as we start off on our bumpy ride to town. It seems like we make it to Maysville in no time at all thanks to the frozen ground. Benjamin takes me straight to my grandmother's house, where he is to spend the night and then take the horse and carriage back home the next day, leaving me with my grandmother until spring. At least, those are the orders my father gave him. Benjamin and I have other plans.

My grandmother invites us in and accepts Benjamin as if he is a white man. We eat our meal together and fill her in on what the plan really is. Benjamin is not going to go home tomorrow, but he is going to enlist as a Union soldier. She is ecstatic.

"We need as many men as we can muster to win this war and put an end to slavery. Owning another is ridiculous. I don't know how I took part in it all those years and how your father can sleep at night, Josephine. I wish I had raised him differently. Living in town and reflecting on my life has shown this old woman how wrong I was all those years ago. It was just our way of life I would always tell myself. I have been trying to right that wrong for a while now. Please, Benjamin, eat some more. You are going to need it."

My grandmother gave Benjamin the best room with the softest linens and wished him a good night.

Why can't everyone have a change of heart like my grandmother so we can all live in peace? I wonder.

Morning comes too quickly. Grandmother's servants prepare a meal fit for a king and even wrap up extras for Benjamin to take with him. My grandmother wishes him farewell and leaves us alone in the parlor.

"I will pray for you every day, Benjamin."

"Please take care of my mother and grandmother."

"You know I will." The tears I had been trying so hard to fight back start to fall.

"Don't cry. When I come back, I will be a free man and we can start our life together."

I smile up at him through blurry eyes. He pulls me in and holds me tightly. Then he kisses me and is gone.

I go straight to my room and pull the cornhusk doll from my trunk, and although no longer a child, I hold it tightly to my chest and pray like I have never prayed before.

"You like the colored gentleman, don't you?" Grandmother

asks as we are taking tea in the parlor the next day.

I smile shyly, staring at my tea cup and unable to look her in the eye.

"He is quite handsome," she says chuckling. "I dare say your lives will not be easy, though, regardless of the outcome of this war."

"I understand."

"Clearly your mother and father will not approve. It will probably send your mother to an early grave if I know her. Do you have any plans?"

"Honestly, none at all. It all depends on the outcome of the war."

BANG! BANG! BANG! "Mother! Mother!"

I jump almost spilling my tea. "Father."

"Don't you worry, I'll take care of him," Grandmother says patting my knee.

I hear the servant open the door and then my father comes barreling into the room out of breath and disheveled.

"Josephine, oh thank God you are safe. When Benjamin didn't come home yesterday, I was afraid something terrible had happened to you." He hugs me quickly. "Where is Benjamin?"

"I don't know. The last I saw he was making his way to the livery stable to get Shadow and the carriage and travel home," I lie.

"I'm going to the stable to see if he even picked up the horse and carriage. I'll be right back," Father says as he rushes out of the house.

I look at my grandmother and she smiles. We sit back down to enjoy our tea until Father returns with news we already know.

"I can't believe this, I just can't believe it," Father mutters as he makes his way into the parlor.

"What has happened, Father?"

"Benjamin never went to get the horse. He never intended to come home. After all that I have done for that boy and he repays me in this way. Your mother is going to be furious."

"Where is the boy, Edward?" Grandmother asks.

"The men at the livery stable said they saw him leave on a boat with the federal army. Seems he enlisted as a soldier. Damn that Lincoln!" he yells, striking his fist on the arm of his chair. "Ruining our way of life is what he is doing."

"The way of life of owning another human being?" Grandmother asks mockingly.

"Don't start, Mother," Father warns harshly.

"Times are changing, Son. I think it is time you change with them."

He stands up and leaves the room quickly.

After a quiet supper, my father says he will be leaving in the morning and that he will leave Shadow in the livery stable and I can come home when I want. I tell him he can expect me the first day of April and not a day later.

My time in town flies by quickly and is a much-needed distraction. I attend church often, a catholic church called Saint Patrick, with a newly acquainted Irish friend, Catherine. Although I do not know what the Reverend Peter McMahon is saying, I enjoy listening to the Latin language and praying silently to myself. Grandmother and I shop often, attend ladies aid meetings, and even squeeze in time for a very comical theatrical performance. I haven't laughed so hard in years.

Sadly, it is the first of April and time to make the trip home. I say goodbye to my grandmother and guide Shadow in the direction of home. Travel is slow due to the previous day's rains having made the roads thick with mud. If I am not careful, Shadow's hooves and the carriage sink, so I try to keep off to the side of the road as much as I can. I see a rather sloppy place ahead and I try to steer Shadow around it, but it is to no avail. My wheels stick and the carriage jolts. I get off the carriage and push it with all my might. Finally, the wheels release with a terrible sucking noise and I almost fall on my face. Luckily, I have sense enough to put my hands out to catch me. I curse under my breath and then immediately say a prayer for forgiveness. My hands, shoes, and the bottom half of my skirt are covered in mud as I climb back into the carriage. Regardless of the terrible road conditions, I make it to our lane in decent time. Home has never looked so inviting as I turn Shadow towards it. I can tell she thinks the same as she picks up speed.

"Almost there, big girl, almost there," I tell her.

She answers with a snort.

"Old Tom comes limping up when we arrive. He helps me out of the carriage and takes Shadow to the stable. I walk wearily up to the front door and inside the house. Mother looks up from the parlor where she is sewing, eyes immediately darting to my dress.

"You are filthy. Are you ever going to grow up and act like a woman? Ann, get her cleaned up before she ruins the rug."

"It's good to see you too, Mother. If you haven't noticed, it rained yesterday and the roads are nothing but mud."

"Well, you don't need to be bringing it in with you."

Not wanting to argue, I allow Ann to guide me to the tub and help me get the heavy, wet petticoats off. *I should have worn a simpler dress during my travels,* I realize too late. The bath water feels good and turns brown as I step in. I could stay in the tub forever, but I hear Father's voice as he comes into the house.

"Where is my beautiful Josephine? How I have missed her," my father queries dramatically.

"I'll be there in a minute, Father."

I dress quickly and make my way to the dining room where my father and mother are talking.

"There she is," my father says as I enter the room. He walks over to me and gives me a big hug. "Did you have a nice time?"

"Yes, I did, thank you."

"This came for you while you were away. It looks like it is all the way from France," he says as he hands me a letter.

Elizabeth, I think. I excuse myself and hurry to my room to read it.

Dear Josephine,

I hope this letter finds you well. I know your country is in a fierce civil war as it has caused many great shortages here, especially cotton. There were talks that France and Britain were going to provide aid to the South. I prayed and prayed they would change their minds and it appeared that the Battle of Antietam, a much-needed victory by the North, turned the tide of the war. This news followed by Lincoln's Emancipation Proclamation helped to persuade France and Britain to steer clear of aiding the South, not only so they would not be supporting what appears to be a lost cause, but also because France and Britain do not want to support slavery. Prayer is very powerful and I will keep praying for you and that the North comes out victorious. God bless you and stay safe.

Yours Cordially,

Elizabeth Julien

I immediately retrieve a piece of parchment and begin to

write to her.

Dear Elizabeth,

It is good to hear from you. I am doing as well as can be expected since my country is at war and some of my loved ones are away. My Aunt Diane is a field nurse for the Northern Army and my brother John is a field surgeon for the Confederates. I worry about them terribly. I had a close call at a skirmish in Augusta. Here we were, minding our own business, when Morgan's Raiders attack the city. It was very frightening and it pains me to say that I had to kill two men to protect myself and another woman. Frederick was one of the men that I killed and the thing that frightens me most is that I really don't feel any remorse for it. I hope you don't think any differently of me. Lincoln's Emancipation Proclamation, as you know, has allowed colored men to enlist in the Union Army. Elizabeth, I helped Benjamin escape the farm and enlist! I don't know where he is now, I can only pray he stays safe.

I hope all is well with you and your family.

Yours Truly,

Josephine

I just finish signing my name and I hear a commotion downstairs. I run down as quickly as I can.

"Josephine, he's been wounded! Oliver's been wounded!" Mary screams through tears as she barrels through the front door.

My heart skips a beat. "Is he okay?"

"I received this letter dated February. Oliver said he was in the Battle of Murfreesboro in Tennessee. He took a musket ball to his arm. Your brother dug it out and told him how to wrap it and how to keep the infection out. Thank goodness no bone was shattered. He said he was going to keep fighting. Josephine, how can he fight with only one good arm? Why would he want to continue fighting?"

"I don't know, Mary. These boys are stubborn, both sides. I am so tired of war. Never knowing if our loved ones are safe. All we can do is continue to pray for these men and pray that the war ends so they can come home. All of them."

"I agree. I don't care who wins any more. I just want Oliver home safe."

Mary stays through supper, and afterwards, we head outside for a walk. The grounds are muddy, but we don't care. It is so nice to walk around outside in the fresh air and forget about the troubles of our country. The slaves are out working the land trying to get it ready for another year of planting, their backs bent and they are singing a low, mournful sounding song. *Hang in there,* I think, *hopefully your lives will belong to you soon.* The sun starts to set and Mary decides to go home.

"Thank you for keeping me distracted for a couple hours. You are lucky you don't have a loved one who is a soldier," she says as she kisses me on the cheek.

"Yes, I am," I manage to say. *If she only knew.*

Old Tom helps her into the buggy and her driver starts the horse home.

With Benjamin filling my thoughts, I make my way around the house to find Ann and Delilah. I find them in their quarters with Frannie. I hug each one of them. I have missed them so. I tell them about Oliver and how I fear something terrible will happen to Benjamin.

"Child," Delilah begins, "We all worry about Benjamin, but we also happy for him. He finally getting to act as a free man and fight against the injustices that have plagued our people for years. If anything happens to him, we will be sad for sure, but we also be happy because we know he died a free man, doing what he want to do and not what the white man force him to do."

"You just keep praying for him, Jo. Keep praying," Ann adds.

"Ann, I'm afraid I am about prayed out," I say as I leave their quarters.

Delilah is right. No matter what happens to Benjamin, he is finally doing what he wants to do. I smile as I climb the steps and head to my room. If the North wins the war, he will always be able to do what he wants to do.

Chapter 31

As I descend the steps, I can hear someone crying in the parlor. I walk in quietly and see my mother sitting on the settee with the newspaper in hand and tears streaming down her face.

"Mother, what happened? Is it John? Why are you crying?" I question her rapidly, alarmed.

"No dear, it's not John. He is okay as far as I know."

"Well, what happened? You never cry. Is it Father? Is something wrong with Father? Please tell me."

"No dear, your father is okay as well. I was reading this paper Edward brought home and it appears that General Stonewall Jackson was shot and killed accidentally by his own men."

"Who won the battle?" I ask.

"A good Confederate man like General Jackson has been killed and all you want to know is who won the battle."

"I am sorry General Jackson has been killed, but I would still like to know who won the battle."

"We won the battle. It was at Chancellorsville, Virginia. They are saying this is General Lee's greatest victory so far. Too bad it has to be tainted by General Jackson's death."

"The Confederates won the battle?" I repeat, defeated.

"Yes, I know, I feel the same way. I am happy we won, but saddened by General Jackson's death."

I walk out of the room. If my mother knew why I was really upset, she would probably kill me on the spot.

"What is this?" Mother yells angrily from the parlor. "Josephine, where are you?"

I freeze. *What did I do now?*

Father comes in from the other room. "What is your mother hollering about?"

"I don't know," I answer.

Mother flies out of the parlor. "Where is she? Where is that wretched whore?"

Father steps in front of me, blocking Mother from getting to me. I have never seen her so angry.

"Charlotte, what is the matter?" Father asks.

She flings a piece of paper at my father, "Read this."

Father begins reading it out loud.

Dearest Jo,

I am a soldier now, although it doesn't seem like it. They have most of us colored folk digging ditches and performing other menial labor. I haven't been in battle yet, but I am itching to fight for my people. There isn't a day goes by that I don't think about you. I have only been gone a few months, but I cannot wait until I can be in your presence as a free man.

Your soldier,

Benjamin

"What does this mean, Josephine?" Father asks as he turns to face me.

"It means she is a filthy whore!" Mother screams hysterically.

"I am nothing of the sort. We are friends and will always be friends. That is all that means."

"Is there anything more between the two of you?" Father

continues.

"No, Father, we have been friends since we were babies and that is where it ends," I lie.

"Charlotte, they have always been friends and we know that. If Josephine says they are nothing more, than I believe her. She knows her place in society and would never stoop to such a low. Would you, Josephine?"

"No, Father, I am appalled by Mother's accusations and disgusted by them," I assure him barely able to catch my breath.

Mother snatches the letter from his hands and begins ripping it up. "Get out of my face, Josephine. I can't bear to look at you right now."

As I am leaving the room, I hear Mother say, "I told you we should have sold that boy years ago."

I don't hear any more. I race out to find Ann and Delilah. I catch sight of them doing the wash with some of the other slave women.

"Benjamin wrote me. He is alive and well. They have him digging ditches and performing other menial labor right now. Oh, I'm so happy he is ok."

"Praise Jesus," Delilah whispers with eyes closed. "Praise Jesus."

"I can't stay, Mother is furious. She found the letter. I am going to hide out in the stable for a while."

The horses whinny as soon as I walk in. I feel so happy that Benjamin is okay that I dance around the barn until I bump against a stall and fall down laughing. I take deep breaths, inhaling the fresh smell of hay and horses. Shadow moves around restlessly in her stall, so I go to her and rub my hand over her soft muzzle.

"Benjamin is safe, Shadow," I whisper. "We need this war to

end so he can come back to us."

She moves her head up and down as if she understands what I am saying and agrees. I wrap my arms around her neck and hug her tightly taking in her smell and feeling the warmth of her on my arms.

I stay for hours hoping that my mother calms down. When I feel it is long enough, I sneak back into the house. I tiptoe to the parlor and peek in. I do not see my mother, but I do see the pieces of letter scattered in the fireplace. I creep in as quickly as I can and begin gathering up the pieces. When I am sure I have them all, I race up to my room. I scatter the pieces out on my desk and begin to piece them back together. I read the letter over and over again and run my hands over the pieces of paper. I know my mother will miss the pieces in the fireplace, so I tiptoe back down to the parlor and reluctantly sprinkle them back into the fireplace.

Chapter 32

News of Gettysburg hits us hard during the hot month of July. The casualties are numerous. I can hardly keep Mary calm as we look every day at the casualty list. Mother weeps again, but not for any of the dead. She weeps only for the Confederate loss. News of General Grant's victory at Vicksburg a day after Gettysburg seems to turn the tide in favor of the Union. Mother weeps again, but I rejoice along with the slaves. Surely the war will be coming to an end soon, I hope.

We receive a letter from Diane one September day. I read it out loud.

Dear Edward,

I hope this letter finds you well. I am currently in Washington, D.C. working at Harewood General Hospital. My duties here require me to change bandages on various wounds ranging from bullet wounds to amputations. I must say I can easily spot gangrene. The smell is horrendous and I fear I will never be able to rid the odor from my nose. Illness here takes over and spreads so quickly. We are constantly washing linens and soldiers trying to keep everything as clean as we possibly can to help limit the spread of these diseases. I am constantly wrapping men's heads with rags of turpentine to kill the lice. I swear some are so infested you can see their hair move. It reminds me of Medusa's snakes! I try to put on a smiling face every day even though there are days I am so exhausted and overwhelmed by illness and death that I want to break down and cry. These men need me and I am glad I can help ease their pain and sorrow. I cannot wait until this war is over so I can come back to Kentucky. I hope you all and our mother are doing well.

Your loving sister,

Diane

P.S. Although you don't like them, President Lincoln and Mary visit the hospital often. They are always able to bring the soldier's spirits up.

"I wish I could help the soldiers like Diane," I say hopelessly.

"You do not want to be there. Didn't you hear all the grotesque things she has to deal with, the smells, the sickness, and lice? What you need to be doing is finding a good man to marry. Even Mary, as shy as she is, got married before you."

"Look around you, Mother. We are at war. All the men are off fighting."

"You'd rather have a dirty slave for your lover anyway," Mother says with absolute disgust.

"Don't start, Mother. You know that is not true," I lie.

I quickly leave the room to avoid any further confrontation. I head to the parlor and grab my knitting needles. If I can't nurse the soldiers, I can at least provide them with plenty of warm wool socks for the upcoming winter.

Chapter 33

Though it is a warm and sunny June day, I feel cold inside. The flowers are letting off wonderful fragrances, but I can no longer smell them. The war ended two months ago and John and Diane have returned, but Benjamin has not. I was so happy on that April day when General Lee surrendered to General Grant, but now I feel that happiness will never come to me again. I continue to stand, staring out across the fields. There are no slaves toiling in them, tending to our crops while singing their sad songs. There are people out there, but they are no longer slaves. They are free men and women who have decided to stay and work for us, because they have nowhere else to go. I try to feel happy for them, but I cannot. My sadness is overwhelming. It hurts me to get out of bed every morning knowing that I will never see him again. If only I knew what happened to him? What if he is wounded somewhere and can't get to me. What if he is calling out to me? I have to find out what has happened to him or I will never rest.

"Josephine, are you just going to stare out at the fields all day?"

I turn around so quickly I almost fall over.

"Benjamin!" I run into his arms, not caring who sees me.

"I'm a free man now," he whispers.

I look up at him and smile. He kisses me.

"What took you so long to come back to me?"

"I was looking for a place for my family to live."

"Did you find a place?"

"Yes, it is in Philadelphia. It is not a very large place, nothing like what you are used to living in, but it will be filled with love, if you still want me?"

"You are all I have ever wanted."

He kisses me again.

"Have you seen Ann and Delilah?" I ask.

"I came to you first."

"Go see them. I will get some things packed."

John, Diane, and even Father is happy to see Benjamin home. My mother is ignoring the fact.

I tell them our plan to move to Philadelphia. Diane immediately wants to help me pack and John says he will drive us to Maysville to catch the train. Father hands me a purse full of money, seemingly knowing that I have already made up my mind, but Mother says nothing. She just stares at the floor with her jaw and fists clenched.

"Goodbye, Mother," I say as I walk out the door.

I climb into the buggy next to Benjamin and smile at Ann and Delilah who are seated next to each other. John starts the horses and we are on our way. I am still in shock. *I finally get to live my life.* I grab Benjamin's hand and squeeze. He looks quite handsome in his uniform. We make it down the lane and out to the road. I am enjoying the sunshine on my face and the breeze in my hair. I close my eyes for a brief moment, taking it all in, until I hear a horse catching up to us at a quick gate. I open my eyes and turn to see my mother coming at full speed on her horse, Lightning. John pulls Shadow to a stop.

"What's wrong, Mother?" John asks.

"I cannot allow this to happen. This whore daughter of mine will not taint our good name. Get out of the buggy, Josephine. I will not have you running off with some filthy negroes."

"I will not, Mother. I love this man and we are going to have a life together."

"You will get out now or I will shoot your precious Benjamin," she says as she pulls a gun.

"No, Mother! The war is over and he is a free man! You will go to jail if you shoot him," John stammers.

"Josephine, this is your last chance. You will get out of that buggy and come with me. Now!" She cocks the gun. "One, two, three." I see her start to squeeze the trigger.

"Mother, no!" I scream as I get up and throw myself in front of Benjamin. I hear the pop of the gun and feel a stinging in my back.

Benjamin looks horrified as he looks at his hands covered in my blood.

"No, Mother! What are you doing?" I hear John scream.

"Don't you help her, John, or I will shoot you too.

Benjamin helps me sit down, then he springs out of the buggy at my mother. I hear another shot and I see Benjamin's body jerk and then sprawl out on the ground.

Ann and Delilah scream and I manage to stumble out of the buggy to Benjamin. My chest feels like it is on fire with every breath I take. Benjamin is clutching his abdomen in agony. I crawl over to him and he takes me in his arms.

"I love you, Benjamin," I manage to gasp.

"I love you, Jo. I always did and I always will."

I feel his breath leave his body just as I allow the darkness to overcome me.

Chapter 34

Present Day Kentucky

"Benjamin," I whisper. I open my eyes to find Maggie and Cecilia staring down at me.

"Oh my gosh, Samantha, are you okay?" Maggie asks.

"I'm fine. Cecilia, where is Benjamin, I mean, Theo?"

"You were right the first time, child," she says smiling at me. "I think you know where he is waiting for you."

I shoot up out of bed and run down the stairs as fast as my legs will carry me. I hurry around the house to the flower gardens and there, standing with his back to me and looking out over the fields just as I had done all those years ago, was Benjamin, or Theo. It doesn't matter what his name is, he is one in the same to me.

"Benjamin, are you just going to stare out at the fields all day?" I ask.

He turns around smiling, "Josephine."

I run into his arms and we hold each other tightly.

"I knew we would find each other again," he says and kisses me on my forehead. "Love has no boundaries."

* * *

"This is the drawing that kick started your dream?" Maggie asks as she gently unfolds the drawing of Benjamin that was tucked away in the copy of Oliver Twist. "Wow, no wonder Theo looked familiar to you. There is quite a resemblance."

"As there should be. That is me in a different time and much younger." Theo answers smiling. "And here is the other half, Josephine."

"Oh my gosh," I exclaim as I take the drawing from Theo. "How did you find this?"

"My friend Eleanor's mother found it one day when she was a child playing in the old slave quarters shortly after her family purchased this farm. She took it to her mother who put it in a safe place. Her mother was very much into preserving the history of this place," Cecilia answers.

"That is amazing. Now we can add the corn husk doll as well as the letters that were under the floor board to this box. What else is in there?" I ask curiously.

"Well, there are the newspaper articles on Josephine and Benjamin's death as well as the trial and hanging of Charlotte," Theo says as he hands the articles to me.

"I read them over and over," blinking back tears. "Cecilia, what happened to Ann and Delilah?"

"From my visions, I learned that they eventually moved to Philadelphia to the house Benjamin had for them with that book and drawing."

"This is just absolutely amazing," Maggie exclaims. "The love you two had for each other was so strong it overcame death and brought you two back together again for a second chance."

I look at Theo blushing and he grabs my hand and squeezes.

"I can still feel the love Benjamin has for Josephine and it is very strong; however, we are different people now. We both agree that we need to get to know each other in this lifetime before we jump into anything relationship wise; however, I feel very confident that things will work out exactly as they should."

"As do I," I chime in smiling.

About the Author

Joanna Bess has tried and accomplished many things: she played professional basketball overseas, achieved 1st degree black belt in Tang Soo Do, was granted a spot on the USA Women's Olympic handball team (which she politely declined), and she can now add published a novel to her list with her debut historical fiction novel *Josephine's Defiance*. She currently resides in Kentucky surrounded by family and friends.

You can connect with me on:

🌐 https://www.joannabess.org

📘 https://www.facebook.com/Joanna-Bess-Author-Page-102109628288629

🔗 https://www.instagram.com/joannabess_author

🔗 https://www.amazon.com/author/joannabess